Mission Space

ISBN 978-1492799801 (sc)
ISBN 978-91-978399-4-5 (pdf ebook)
Also available on Kindle

First printed in Swedish 2012

Support with translation and publishing: Aaron Rose, USA

Other books in English by Mariana Stjerna:
Agartha – The Earth's Inner World (2013)
On Angels' Wings (2013)
The Bible Bluff (2013)

SoulLink Publisher
www.SoulLink.se
info@SoulLink.se

Mariana Stjerna

Mission Space

SoulLink Publisher

Dedication

This book is primarily dedicated to my two daughters, Tina and Louise, whom I earnestly hope will strive to read Mother's waffle! I love you dearly!

A further dedication is to my dear friends, whose unfailing support and encouragement has constantly kept me going – namely the lovely couple Inga and Cagga Levander – not forgetting their son, David. Many thanks for the interest you have shown and all the help given!

Last but not least, I should like to convey my fondest thanks to darling Chris, my seven-year-old miniature poodle, for his unceasing involvement and devotion within my close vicinity.

Jan Fridegård (1897-1968) grew up as a farm laborer and tried several professions before the debut of his writings: *One Night in July* (1933). His autobiographical novel trilogy about Lars Hård is perhaps his finest work. The death of his father aroused a latent interest in the supernatural, which came to be reflected in *The Tower Rooster* (1941).

Contents

Foreword

It hadn't been my intention to write any further books about Jan and Lydia. When the Swedish version of the book *Agartha – The Earth's Inner World* (SoulLink Publisher, Sweden, 2013) had been released, I had enlightened my readers about the Earth's inner hollows and the bounteous wealth of this Realm, called Agartha. In my professional capacity as an authoress I naturally cannot present absolute proof of the existence of this place, even if there are some contemporary people walking the Earth who claim actually to have been there.

Furthermore, it would entail a great risk to Agartha's continued equilibrium if the Earth's populace as a whole suddenly became aware of its existence since, regrettably, we humans usually consider all that is alien to us to be a potential threat. This unhealthy attitude has to be changed in a quiet and amicable manner, without undue quarrel and dogmatic denial.

Mission Space came about specifically to elucidate the fact that advanced, cultivated civilizations do exist out in Space, who would like to make contact with Earth in order to teach us how we can improve our lives through love, co-operation, light, and harmony. The latter are the essential elements, so sadly lacking on our dear planet, which we desperately need to learn to develop.

I believed this book was to be a sort of farewell parting from Jan Fridegård, but I was wrong in my assumption, for I have been inspired to write yet another manuscript: "Visiting Unknown Worlds – An Exploration of My Inner Space." This is about my experiences regarding my own inner space and even includes a little autobiographical material. However, Jan and Lydia have now declined accepting any further commissions, laying claim to other matters taking precedence. It is therefore with some regret that my Janne-inspired books finally come to an end. Furthermore, this authoress confesses to having reached a venerable age no longer permitting the pen to flow along paper quite as fleetingly as in former days.

I wish finally to profusely thank all my readers for having so devoutly perused my books. Perhaps our paths may cross again in another dimension … no, sorry, on another frequency, of course. Until then, dear reader, please promise that you will endeavor not to be afraid. Fear destroys all the goodness within us and all the best we've managed to build up throughout the years. Fear eradicates our opportunities to finding true bliss, faith, and love – above all, Love. There really is nothing to be afraid of – unless you happen to bump into a hungry lion in the woods at night … so avoid that!

With an amiable chuckle and a mischievous glint in the eye, I say, "Farewell!" … But, you never know, that might perhaps just mean "Till we meet again!"

– Mariana Stjerna

1. The Mission

Jan Fridegård called out to Mariana:

<*Jan*> "Hello, hello; are you there?"

<*Mariana*> "Yes, yes! Where have you been? I have written a book about Agartha – this time without you at my side! I have missed you so!"

<*Jan*> "I'm glad to hear it! For now I am here. I, too, have been in Agartha; I had a great experience while I was there, so, too, on Sirius – I can tell you! I had been sent on a mission to both Sirius and the Pleiades – also, last but not least, Andromeda. So what do you think about that?"

<*Mariana*> "Please tell, Janne; do tell all! Shall we write a new book; your fifth one?"

<*Jan*> "Exactly, my dearest old medium. Once again, it is time … I really do have so very much to tell."

<*Mariana*> "Will we manage in time? Before the world collapses, I mean?"

<*Jan*> "We can but try. You know how the pace quickens, when I have much on my heart to tell! The world will continue its existence a while longer, but for the moment it is the readers who are of prime importance. They also will live on – and when danger threatens I shan't fail to shriek out and say it's time to flee. So just listen to your old friend who speaks through your ears."

<*Mariana*> "But I am in the process of writing a children's book about Agartha."

<*Jan*> "Well, can't that wait awhile? I don't know how long I will be permitted to remain on this wavelength, so I really wish to start RIGHT NOW. In fact, my dear Mariana, we have already begun!"

As usual, I, Jan, had been called in to my very dear friend, Melchizedek. Exactly when, regarding our Earthly concept of time, I cannot say – since such time does not exist and cannot be measured in other Worlds. Suffice to say that I was out relaxing in my own pleasant garden, leisurely taking a well-deserved nap in my armchair. I was enjoying the heavenly spherical music, vibrating in the still, balmy air of the tranquil surroundings I had myself created and called "home." But when duty calls, there is a sudden awakening, likened to the crashing of thunderous drums and trumpet blasts. The otherwise so unobtrusive, gentle, and kindly spirit, Lydia, arriving together with a few child-angels who were bashing away at various instruments, presumably purposefully to annoy me, caused this rude interruption.

Lydia, who seems to become more and more beautiful every time I see her, took hold of both my hands and dragged me up on my feet, saying, "Jan, we are to embark on a new adventure together. Melchizedek informs us that we must hurry to him – as you well know, it's urgent in the spirit world!"

A cascade of laughter followed the latter while she beckoned the child-angels to leave. Within a second, the great Master Melchizedek stood before us. He embraced us warmly and indicated that we should sit down opposite him.

"Welcome, my dear adventurers!" he kindly announced. "I have an assignment best suited for you two to carry out. It is a mission to an extraordinary place that will not be found on the human maps of the Earth. I'm thinking of sending the pair of you to Agartha, Earth's Inner World, which most certainly exists on both physical and non-physical levels. I need your help at both levels, consequently necessitating that you must be able to swiftly materialize and dematerialize your bodies between the physical and non-physical states. It may further involve a trip to both Sirius B and the Pleiades. Fear or resistance is not permitted, which goes without saying as far as the two of you are concerned. The venture commences immediately, after you have been informed about the nature and purpose of the mission."

Why would we protest? This mission seemed to be tailor-made for us. We were both most proud to be chosen to participate in something like this. So it was with joy and excitement that we received the nature and purpose of our mission. And now, my dear readers, you are to join me on breath-taking travels – both inside Earth and galactic. Welcome!

2. Welcome to Agartha!

"Naturally, I've been aware of Agartha's existence, but never dwelt on the thought," I explained to Lydia, once we had been given all the information and instructions we required. We took hold of one another's hands and stood in the midst of my beautiful garden, in which the birdsong was almost deafening. We had made up our minds that we would start off with Agartha – so to Agartha we went.

It's always a question of moments – quite literally – whenever we transport ourselves, no matter how far the distance. We simply shut our eyes – and quickly open them again! That's about it! But readers will surely think this is magic, so I regret I am unable to give a detailed account of such instantaneous flight. Lydia stood before me in her pale blue, full-length, flimsy frock, wearing a hairband of blue and silver, bearing exquisite, dazzlingly cut jewelry, just like the moment before. Seemingly I, too, looked the same in my short white tunic with gold belt and tight-fitting, white trousers – this was plain to read in her smiling eyes. However, our surroundings were entirely new.

We were standing on a mound, or small hill. Immediately beneath us was a little village, embedded amongst a mass of trees. The houses were round and singularly constructed, glistening with precious gems, just like the narrow pathways that weaved their way in between them. A little farther afield, we spied the sun-spangled water and felt the delightful heat of the sun penetrating our bodies.

Apparently we had physical bodies, and evidently this was a part of Agartha.

"Surely this cannot be the capital city of Agartha?" pondered the historian, Lydia. "This must be a village on the outskirts of Telos, the town situated closest to the surface of the Earth. It is here that humans from the upper surface come, if they happen to land underneath. There

15

are many descending paths here, so we have learned. I believe this to be close to the great entrance on Mount Shasta, for it is very like our type of nature. Just look at the trees and glistening lake over there."

"Well, perhaps not the houses, but possibly the wonderful nature, apart from the gems," I conceded. "We do not use precious stones quite so liberally."

"Here they are in great abundance," my most knowledgeable companion informed us, smiling. "The mountains are oozing with them. Shall we move along, lazybones? We're not here purely to stand around and stare. Look, here's a stairway, so it looks like others often walk here."

The stairway even had a banister. The steps appeared to be carved right into the rock, and dense shrubbery grew on both sides, all the way down. Some of the bushes were in bloom and others bore berries. We tiptoed down, drinking in the soothing summer fragrance of the shrubs and basking in the tranquil beauty that enveloped us.

Finally reaching the bottom of the steps, we appeared to be standing on something rather like a fairly large, marble courtyard, which led out directly towards the village. There was only one exit, so it was just a case of following the path it took. We didn't see any people, but the houses seemed taller than when seen from above; the odd thing about them was not only the round shape, but they also had no roofs.

Lydia stretched out her arms and danced around; humming a happy tune, she pulled me into the dance. The smooth marble of the courtyard, or terrace, was particularly conducive to dancing – but we were interrupted by a clear voice, saying, "What do you think you're doing? This is no time for dancing, and we certainly shouldn't be dancing here. Who are you? Have you come down from the top of the hill?"

We abruptly halted. The shrill voice belonged to a young girl, almost a child, possibly about twelve years of age. She was tall and slim, with wavy hair that was almost white and blew around in the gentle, summer breeze. Her face was beautiful, and when she smiled she exposed a perfect row of pearl-white teeth. She wore a flouncy, pink skirt with a matching-colored, shimmering blouse. She spoke in a tongue we understood, as was usual when we were on our travels.

"We are sorry if we are trespassing here," I apologized, bowing courteously. "We have come from a foreign land on another planet and just wished to look around."

"We have heard much about your fair country and were rather curious to see it; we've only just arrived," Lydia hastily added. "We love to dance. Whenever I see something beautiful, it makes me want to sing and dance."

"It sounds as though you are one of us," the girl said, laughing. "My name is Nelsea. I live there!" She pointed to the house closest to them. "Come with me and meet my father and mother; you perhaps are hungry if you have been travelling long."

The moment she uttered the word "hungry," I felt an instant hunger and thirst. This indicated that we now had human bodies and that these were humans we were meeting. Melchizedek indeed knew whither he had sent us. Lydia winked at me; she obviously was aware of the situation, too. We followed along to the house behind the girl, who had a peculiarly compelling, floating gait.

"Goodness, how compactly you tread on the gravel!" exclaimed Nelsea, as she glanced back at us. "You are not allowed to do so here; one can easily tell you are strangers here. What a stroke of luck that it was such a short walk!"

As we arrived at the building, the front door stood open. It looked like a perfectly ordinary door, made out of some sort of light-colored, transparent material, but I didn't have time to make a thorough check before we found ourselves inside the most astonishing house. There was no entrance hall or cloakroom. There was just one great big room – an enormous, circular room – with a very high ceiling, since there was no roof. The circular room had no inner dividing walls, but a couple of areas were partitioned off with screens. Nelsea took us directly to one partition, where there was a comfortable suite, also made of some indescribable material. Two people were sitting there, presumably Nelsea's parents. They immediately stood up when we appeared. Nelsea seemed more to float rather than walk up to them.

"I found these two out on the plateau," she explained. "They come from the upper Earth and another planet; from Space, perhaps."

I scrutinized Nelsea's parents while we warmly greeted them with smiles, which were instantly reciprocated. The woman hugged Lydia and the man gave me a welcome embrace; his body felt firm and muscular, just like an ordinary human being.

"Welcome to Agartha and the town of Telos, beneath Mount Shasta!" he said. "We are accustomed to visitors, living as we do so closely to the Earth's surface. My name is Boron and this is my wife, Tulli."

Both of them were extremely tall and looked very young – far too young to have a twelve-year-old daughter. Boron must have been well over six and a half feet tall; he was fair-skinned with curly brown hair. Tulli was just a little shorter than Boron, with long, straight, thick, fair hair that hung in a thick plait all the way down her back.

Their clothes were simple and straight-cut, rather like shirts, but both of them wore the most elegant jewelry. They bade us sit on one of the soft, shimmering green sofas.

"The Pilgrim!" exclaimed Madam Tulli and stared at me. "Just think if he who calls himself Jan is the Pilgrim!"

"If so," soothed her husband, "he wouldn't have female company. I've never heard of the Pilgrim ever travelling with anyone other than himself; although I believe he has a dog with him. My dear wife, we have Space visitors in Inner Earth, for which we are to be happy and grateful for – with no allusions to the Pilgrim. Admittedly, he has done only good things up until now, but one never knows …"

"And who, may I ask, is the Pilgrim?" I inquired, sensing the importance of the question.

The couple looked meaningfully at one another while Nelsea curled up in her armchair. Finally Boron answered, "He calls himself the Pilgrim, and we know him by no other name. He wanders all over Agartha and is becoming well known to everyone. He is no evil person; on the contrary he is very wise and good, but he never stays in the same place more than fleetingly. He has healed many who have needed help, for even though we neither have plagues nor disease, accidents happen, just as they do up above." He pointed upwards, towards the great hole where the roof normally would have been. "He explains to those who do not understand things and informs those who have not heard – he just suddenly appears where he is most needed – and many have seen him wandering around our streets, without his feet touching the ground. Naturally, we are most curious to find out who he really is."

"Did he simply turn up here one day?" inquired Lydia.

"Yes," Tulli answered, "That is precisely what he did. A child tumbled down a precipice while playing a somewhat wild game. The poor little thing was lying at the bottom of the steep slope, without moving. She had a rather nasty wound on her head that was bleeding badly. All of a sudden he was there, the Pilgrim. He touched the child and the bleeding immediately ceased. A short while later the girl was able to stand up and walk about. But the Pilgrim had already vanished before she could thank him. Similar things have occurred in several places."

"It sounds as though he is a very good man," I commented. "He could be a great Master in disguise, wandering around, doing good."

"Or a spy, doing good while he's really spying on us," disputed Nelsea. Her father raised a warning finger.

"Here we think well of everyone," he declared gravely, "right up until we are able to prove anything to the contrary. But enough of this, for you have yet the opportunity of seeing your way around our beautiful land, which I will gladly show you. When we have eaten, I shall guide you around, if you two are agreeable to this."

Both Lydia and I gratefully accepted this proposal. Madam Tulli served a most delicious vegetable dish with homemade bread (where in the world did they do their baking?). We carried no luggage, since we were proficient at being able to precipitate, i.e., acquire whatever we wished by power of thought. Nelsea asked permission to join us, so once the meal was concluded, we found ourselves climbing up into one of Agartha's well-known vehicles, something like an open-top car without wheels, called a hovercraft – and it certainly hovered exceedingly well!

3. By Hovercraft to Porthologos

To hover On Angels' Wings is something I am used to, but this experience was entirely new to me. It gave neither the sensation of an airplane nor a helicopter, but possibly a bit like travelling close to the ground in a hot-air balloon. There we sat in a box with six narrow, upholstered seats facing the same way, positioned in three of rows of two, behind one another. Above us was a collapsible roof that could be pulled over in bad weather, although it mostly was fine in these climes. On this day, the sun was shining brightly and the calm, sapphire-blue water beneath us glittered as though spangled with millions of diamonds. The hovercraft glided close above the water, occasionally hopping up to avoid a sudden wave that disturbed the otherwise serene surface.

The lake we sailed over was not large, or at least one could view land in all directions, and we soon found ourselves right above a real big dipper of a beach. The sand dunes went up and down so much that our vehicle kept a steady six feet above them. Shellfish and small creatures moved like patterns in the sand, but when I looked up, I could see homely woodland ahead of us, which indicated that the sea landscape was coming to an end. This made me happy, since I am an incorrigible landlubber and have never really understood others' longing for the sea. Perhaps my upbringing as a farm-laborer boy in my latest human incarnation explains this. I still feel very much at home in the farming areas out in the countryside, amongst the cows, sheep, and horses. I adore the smell of stables and the fresh breeze of meadows during the harvest, interspersed with cornflowers and poppies. In short, farmhand Janne is still very much a part of me, ambling around the farmyard in sturdy wooden clogs, just like the elves that mother used to talk about.

Boron, who was sitting behind me, bent forward and patted my shoulder. "We are on the way to our prestigious library, situated several miles under the ground you see here. It is called Porthologos and is renowned for housing all knowledge in existence."

I was silent. This sounded rather boastful, but Lydia immediately chattered away, asking a mass of questions: "What does the library look like? Does it contain every single book in the world, in all languages – even Indian? English? Swedish? Are there dictionaries in all languages? And can one borrow books, just like on the surface?"

"We don't normally lend books out as you do," said a grinning Boron. "Quite simply because books here do not mean the same thing as the ones you are used to. Even if there are books, you won't find them standing on shelves; they can only be supplied on demand. The library mediates knowledge in a different way – soon you will see."

The hovercraft had slowed down and was about to land. It landed softly and gracefully, just as though setting a fragile object down on a table. We swiftly found ourselves in a grove with tall, lush, blossoming trees, and ahead of us lay a mountain – or something that likened to a mountain, even though in patches it glittered with precious jewels. There was a door into the mountain, and Boron beckoned to us to climb out of the hovercraft and follow him. The door looked as though it was made of horizontal tree trunks, making it blend in with the rest of the woodland. It couldn't have been very heavy, because when Nelsea ran up to it, it easily swung open automatically. I supposed she must have pressed a button somewhere.

I took hold of Lydia's hand and walked up to the door. Boron had gone ahead of us, down a stone staircase into a hall with several doors leading off. We followed after, and I heard Nelsea's boisterous giggles behind us. I wondered whether we were being led right into a trap – which was probably a forbidden thought in this place.

"I trust you are not afraid?" teased Boron, laughing as he opened a door. "I can assure you that this is a most delightful place – like you would call a cinema, in fact."

"You seem to know a great deal about the world above," I blurted out.

"I have visited it a few times," came the reply. "But I do know that the two of you are not from there. I wonder which planet you are from."

"We actually come from another dimension," was Lydia's reply. "But we have both lived lives on the surface before existing there. The two of us are now to discover new places that human beings ought to know about. They refuse to acknowledge Agartha and they deny the existence of all forms of life in the Universe, other than their own on Earth. It is our task to change their attitude. Can you help us?"

"I can certainly show you around here and a few other places close to Telos, but Agartha is divided into different zones, wherein both three-dimensional and five-dimensional beings exist. We are three-dimensional for the time being, by our own choice. Telos is something of a bridge over to the surface Earth, and contains a great mixture of human-like beings, most of whom are, of course, Agarthans, born and bred here. However, we probably know more about Outer Space than you do. Go in there and you will understand better."

He indicated with his hand towards an open door, which we then entered and found ourselves standing before a sort of amphitheater. Boron continued with his guided tour.

"What you see here is a history book!" he exultantly explained. "Is there anything in particular you wish to know?"

"Oh yes, indeed!" cried Lydia the historian, jumping up with sheer delight. Boron led us down to the front row in the stalls, right in front of the great stage. "I have always wondered how Cleopatra's first meeting with Antony went – such great, passionate lovers that they were to be!"

I tittered quietly to myself; this was typical Lydia! It would have to be love that she wanted to have confirmed. But I barely had time for this thought to enter my head before the huge stage before us suddenly filled with gently lapping waves, sighing winds, glorious sunshine over glittering water, music, and singing. A magnificent sloop glided slowly along, exactly the type of single-mast sailing boat I had seen illustrated in history books. The sparkling golden draperies and billowing red cushions gave the impression of almost intrinsic beauty, reaching out so gracefully. Here was, of course, Cleopatra, I thought. Her clothing was sparse, but her shiny, long black hair was set up in a truly magnificent style, with ribbons of pearls and gold, plus all manner of such things that a simple man is quite unable to describe these days.

To my sheer delight, her frock was pleated, but transparent. Lydia pulled at my shirtsleeve and whispered, "Don't look!" But of course I did.

Another sloop drew near from the opposite direction. It looked more war-like and was in a convoy of several other boats. At the bow stood an athletically-built man, who obviously was Mark Antony. He was extremely good-looking, I thought, with his dark brown, shoulder-length hair and wearing a golden cape, nonchalantly flung over his shoulders. He had even features, a straight but powerful nose, and dark brown eyes – more or less as one would imagine him to have been. The two sloops met and caught one another. Antony jumped over to the beautiful Cleopatra, falling to his knees before her – she was, after all, a Queen.

As quickly as this scene had appeared as in a theater with seemingly live people, so also it just vanished into thin air.

"These are holographic pictures," explained Boron. "Your kind is not yet as advanced, but we have had this technology for hundreds of years."

"In other words, you're a bit behind," giggled Nelsea. Her father cast her a warning glance.

"You can see whatever historical picture you like," he continued. "I'd like to show you how, teaching with them. The children and youths are also given holistic education, but then there is a history narrator included in the picture."

"It seems to be great fun attending school here," said Lydia, sighing. "I think of how tedious our method of education is, using books oozing with dates to be memorized."

"We shall move on," said Boron, who had already risen to his feet and started up the same stairway they had earlier descended. We followed along behind him, with Nelsea hopping and skipping along like a little fawn.

When we arrived at the same hall, with all its doors, Nelsea happily opened another door, this time leading out into a garden. There were tables and chairs there, and Boron invited us to sit down.

"You have seen how teaching is conducted here," he said. "When it comes to zoology, we have a magnificent zoo that houses all types of animals, even the dangerous ones."

"Do you have any dragons?" interrupted Lydia, with eyes shining, and I chimed in with her; it was an exciting question to ask.

"Of course," responded Boron, quite unperturbed. "We have dragons both in the zoo and in the wilderness. When they were hunted almost to extinction on the surface, they fled here. We taught trainers and dragon-riders, and consequently they have remained here. It has become trendy to write about dragons on the surface. We have been spending a great deal of time and effort in inspiring writers there, in order that what they write will be accurate."

"Are there both good and evil dragons?" I inquired. "Just like good and evil humans?"

Boron shook his head. "Evil is banned here," he declared. "It is not tolerated, in either animals or people. Of course, we are allowed a bit of harmless banter – to joke and tease – but only when exercised in the manner of good will. Youngsters have become a little too free in their speech lately." He looked sternly at his daughter, but she just giggled.

"You don't really need to see so very much more of Porthologos," he added. "There are other things I would like to show you. Porthologos is endless and works only by a living pattern. Either by holographic pictures or through reality – that is to say, as you would interpret it. We, however, see it differently; but since you come from another planet, you perhaps understand us better?"

Both Lydia and I nodded emphatically. We followed after Boron and his happily scampering daughter out into the garden, up some steps, and through a passage – and in an instant we were standing in the forest, with the hovercraft awaiting us.

"Our very own Bentley!" sighed Lydia, as she seated herself comfortably in the vehicle. "I wonder where it will take us now?"

25

4. The Temple –
An Enormously Great Jewel

We then hovered high up, way above the treetops. The sun shone just as brightly and it was still warm, but not hot. I started to feel pangs of human hunger in my stomach, and I was also thirsty. I glanced at Lydia. She pointed to her tummy and mouth, to make me understand that her human, physical side was also beginning to make itself known.

Boron turned around and smirked, knowingly. "You are hungry and thirsty!" he declared. "We can soon put that right."

The hovercraft dived downwards, seemingly straight into the middle of the forest. In contrast to the last time we landed, now we came down with a bump, since we were travelling at a greater speed. It looked like a grove, but the ground was even and we were pleased to step out of our jumpy vehicle.

"I do apologize for not managing to handle the landing better," said Boron, laughing. "Nelsea was behaving a bit mischievously. Anyway, there are chairs and tables here; please sit yourselves down and you shall soon be given both food and drink."

And sure enough, bang in the center of the grove stood a most inviting, rustic table, made out of what looked like thick branches that hadn't even been planed down. The seats were comprised of two sturdy benches, made out of the same material.

"I bet you've never encountered a cafeteria like this before!" guffawed Boron, as we all sat down. He murmured a couple of inaudible words (I think) and in an instant an enormous serving dish, also made of wood, appeared before us on the table. A most appetizing stack of sandwiches (but none with ham) was piled high on the plate, and Boron bade us to dive in and eat. Wooden goblets also suddenly stood on the table before us, filled with a delightfully palatable drink, which I later learned was Agarthan beer. To round the meal off, we ate delicate little Agarthan biscuits, which were filled with some sort of exquisite creamy mixture.

After we had eaten and drunk our fill, we clambered back into the Bentley-vehicle. "I haven't seen a single cow!" exclaimed Lydia, as we once again rose high up in the sky. "So where do you get the cream in those lovely biscuits from?"

The father and daughter's eyes met and, as usual, Nelsea started to giggle more and more loudly. Finally she broke out in uncontrollable shrieks of laughter. However, Boron kept his composure, although he almost smirked when he replied, "It is our opinion that you keep your livestock in captivity. You use them and furthermore steal the milk that is intended to nourish their young. We do have cattle here, all the various breeds that you have up above, only down here we consider them to be our personal friends and they are permitted to wander and graze freely in the pastures. The very idea of drinking or using their milk to our own ends is quite unthinkable – even comical! The sap of certain plants is milk-like with a most pleasing taste and may be whisked to the consistency of cream. It's as simple as that."

"It ought to be that simple for us, too." I felt a sense of great relief, having heard about their protection of the cattle. I, who had milked, washed, and brushed the cows back home, had never liked milk, with perhaps the exception of double cream. To instead be able to obtain it from a plant, really ought to be introduced on Earth. The most astonishing things were revealed to us. What surprise was in store for us next? We were about to find out.

Following the refreshment break, we were once again sitting in our luxury wheel-less vehicle, whizzing through the air in no time. Having passed through some thick clouds, we soon landed again. Boron explained that the clouds sometimes hung fairly near the ground, especially high up in the hills, which was why the hovercraft was forced to drive straight through the woolly, downy, cushion that a cloud acted as. It wasn't really dangerous – a bit like going out in a thick fog – but radar didn't work inside the cloud, so the hovercraft had to disconnect its engine to idling (if it actually had any sort of engine). Anyhow, we did manage to make our way out of the downy cushion fairly swiftly, only to dive into the next one – and so it continued for quite some time, but finally we glided down from cloud-veiled treetops and began our descent to the ground.

An incredibly beautiful building overshadowed our vehicle, but all the glistening rays reflecting from its bejeweled surface served to break up the shadow.

"That's exactly how a temple should look, if I had my way!" I delightedly exclaimed, and Lydia grabbed hold of my arm for support as she stared up at the sparkling cupola. It looked just like one enormous, great, fabulous jewel that stood before us, which we gazed upon in utter amazement.

"This type of building cannot be found anywhere in all history," she whispered, wiping a few tears of joy away from her pale, soft cheek. "This must be the absolutely most beautiful thing I have ever seen. Dare we go inside, or do you think we will be disappointed if we do?"

I thought it unlikely, so in we went. Since churches and cathedrals were not supposed to exist in Agartha, I really did wonder what secret this magnificent building held. It was equally exquisite on the inside as out and full of beautiful paintings and stained glass. There were no long pews or altars, as found in the churches we were familiar with, but instead several lounge areas with sofas and armchairs grouped all around the entire glimmering, shimmering chamber that dazzled our eyes. One or more people, all of whom appeared to be deep in prayer or meditation, engaged some of the lounge areas. Flames arose from something akin to candles, gently flickering in the draught caused by our passing by. There was no altar that I could make out, although one might say the whole of the chamber was like one enormous altar. Out of the blue came faint music. I can't say what sort of music it was or from whence it came, but it went straight into the heart and soul, penetrating all one's deepest emotions. We didn't have the strength to stand and listen, so we sat down in one of the sofas in the middle of the room. At this point even Nelsea kept silent – in fact, seemingly reverent.

"This is a place where specially selected helpers come," whispered Boron. "One comes here whenever one is in need of psychiatric help of any kind or has specific questions to ask. See the helpers over there? They wear either orange- or indigo-colored cloaks. One of them is coming over to us now."

As it happened, it was a slightly older gentleman who walked up to us. He was tall, like they all were, fair-haired, and with a pleasant loving expression about his face. He smiled kindly.

"Welcome, dear visitors from the surface!" he said softly. "My name is Lionor. Have you come here as tourists, or are you in need of help?"

"You might say as a sort of tourist," I replied. "And we are not from the surface, but from another dimension. We bring greetings!" I pronounced a word that Melchizedek had told me would open doors for us. It evidently worked, for the helper bowed deeply in reverence to us.

"What is it you wish to know about Agartha?" he asked.

"I wonder whether you have one solitary religion here or if there are the same assorted denominations as on the surface," I inquired.

"Yes, what is your belief?" Lydia chimed in.

"In the whole of Agartha there is but one faith," responded Lionor. "We have only one God, First Source, for all life on this entire planet. It is a Love Being – or Love Source, as we usually say. It is not only the God of people, but also of animals. Those who cannot accept the Laws of Love relinquish their right to remain here and will be immediately exiled, either to the surface or to some other planet where their beliefs fit. Consequently, we never experience the religious conflicts people on the surface have to struggle with. We live in constant peace and harmony, sending out Love to all dimensions."

"How absolutely wonderful!" sighed Lydia. "The surface humans of Earth could learn much from you."

"Quite so," smiled Lionor. "This is precisely what will come to pass, once the Earth has completed its transition, which won't be long."

"So you are aware of the great dilemma the Earth currently is struggling with?"

Although this was a rhetorical question, Lionor replied, "We are very much aware of all that happens on the surface. There are such horrors, but we take joy in revealing our existence and letting it be known that we are here and willing to help the surface dwellers. We really can. When the great change befalls the Earth, we will be there, helping. Those who will not accept us or listen to what we have to say will have to decide their own fate by choosing another planet to move to where their views are accepted."

"I think we have now spoken of the future quite long enough," interjected Boron. "We shall now continue our expedition in the sunshine. If you will excuse us, Lionor. We can come back later, if my guests so wish."

Lionor respectfully bowed deeply once again and did not rise from his bowed position until after we had left the chamber.

5. An Interesting Acquaintanceship

When we had gone out through the door, we turned to look back and admire the architectural work of art before our eyes. Just as we were expressing our admiration out loud, we heard a voice saying, "Greetings to you, Lydia and Jan!"

Our hovercraft was parked near the temple, and next to it stood a man with a dog. The man was dressed in an off-white cape with a golden belt around his waist. From the belt hung a mass of objects, all in gold. He looked about middle-aged; his hair was almost white but his face was young-looking with sharp features. He had brightly shining, deep blue eyes. The dog resembled a golden-retriever, only it was almost completely white-haired and had a wide collar of gold.

Somewhat taken aback, we greeted the stranger. Boron looked hesitant, as though he ought to introduce the man, without really knowing who he was. Finally it was Lydia who broke the momentary silence, "Are you the one known as the Pilgrim?" she asked, "And what's the name of your lovely dog?"

"The dog is called Lissa, and yes, I am indeed the one known as the Pilgrim," replied the man, grinning slightly. "I had received news that you had arrived in Agartha and I wished to welcome you. There is so much to discover here and much for human beings to learn. You come from another dimension, have temporarily taken physical forms, and wish to learn all you can about Agartha. I would be honored to show you around, if you have no other plans."

"I am their guide at the moment," said Boron. "But I am more than pleased to take a break and return home. I want you to know, Jan and Lydia, that you always are most welcome back to see us whenever you so wish."

Lydia threw herself at Boron's neck to hug him and Nelsea fluttered into the hovercraft like some, giant, pink-colored butterfly. In an instant both she and her father vanished. There we were, left standing outside the most beautiful temple in the world, in the company of the rather remarkable Pilgrim and his equally remarkable dog.

"These are our friends, Lissa," said the man. "Greet!" The dog first went up to Lydia, and second to me, with its head bowed and right paw lifted. Then it returned to its master's side. The Pilgrim indicated to us to stand perfectly still, and then he blew a little pipe that gave out a whistle. A hovercraft hovered out of the nearby wood and landed beside us; it was golden, with a roof that was all glittery-gold.

"I usually hike around," he declared, "but when I have guests, we use this. Please take a seat and we shall travel to a most interesting place."

We hopped up into the vehicle without saying a word. It felt like dreaming in a dream. The Pilgrim smiled kindly at us the whole time and the hovercraft floated gently and comfortably up in the air.

"I could have transported us by some other method," continued the Pilgrim, "but then you wouldn't have had the advantage of viewing the wonderful Agarthan countryside, which right here is similar to some areas in the Nordic Earth regions. The difference here is the enormous range of plants, since the existing vegetation encompasses all species of plants on Earth since the beginning of time. This is why it is strictly forbidden to pick or pull up any of the plants; as far as we are concerned, all of them are what you would call 'rare.'"

"This being so, it does seem strange that the place isn't completely overgrown," I responded, somewhat surprised, "One would reasonably suppose the entire countryside to consequently be one enormous great jungle of wildly tangled vegetation."

The Pilgrim smirked. "Nature regulates itself," he responded politely. "The King of Nature, Peter Pan, does not only exist in the Nature on the surface, but also here. With him follows all the Elementals. There we have our 'Head Gardeners.' Consequently, we need never worry, because we can rely on all life being well nurtured and protected."

"But what do you do with the dolphins?" I interjected, having suddenly remembered all the ghastly things I had heard about the dolphins in the seven seas on Earth.

These are of so horrifying a nature that I would prefer not to go further into it in this book. However, those who wish to learn more may find information readily available on the Internet. The vicious slaughtering, wicked animal cruelty, and evil these wonderful creatures had been subjected to are beyond all comprehension – and it was for this reason I brought up the question of the dolphins.

"We love and revere our dolphins," replied the Pilgrim. "They are wiser than humans. If any danger befalls them, we immediately go to their assistance. Natural accidents can happen, but we are used to dealing with such and have fantastic, curative natural remedies. Regrettably, we are unable to do anything for the ones that live on the surface, other than to heal them once they arrive here. Some that are not so badly wounded are able to go straight into the sea here, and we keep watch over them."

The hovercraft landed slowly on the long-stretching sandy beach. We disembarked. Dolphins came into view, swimming right up onto the sand, where people gathered around them. Children petted these great aquatic beings, and it looked as though the dolphins cuddled them back. People were feeding them small fish, and the whole wonderful picture was one of reciprocal Love and delight – which I did so wish one could see the same on the surface, too.

The Pilgrim gave out a little laugh. "Well, Jan, are you convinced now? Here the Love of animals is one of the very first things a child learns. I have a dog, my beloved Lissa, because most of us here have a pet. We can learn a great deal from our pets."

"But I thought you weren't from here," I retorted.

"Why should that matter?" was his reply. "I can go along with anything in the name of Love, wherever I might happen to be."

"So can I!" exclaimed Lydia, who was sitting in the sand, with Lissa's big head resting on her knee. "We are having such a lovely conversation, and your dog is telling me lots of things, Pilgrim!"

"I've brought you here to show you something," announced our new guide, whereupon Lissa immediately ran to his side; it was just as though she understood all he said. He beckoned to us to follow him, so we tiptoed after him as lightly as we could on the wet, compressed sand. It was just like at home, I thought – but very soon I discovered it was very different indeed.

We had passed several families playing and exercising on the wide stretch of sandy beach, when all of a sudden it became silent. There was no one in sight; it was as though we had entered a vacuum without walls, with the gentle splashing of the sea waves on one side. The Pilgrim and Lissa hurried on, and we simply kept pace behind, since there was no alternate path to take, other than straight on. In my own mind I decided to call this place a "sea-tunnel," since I have a passion for giving everything a name.

All of a sudden the Pilgrim and his dog came to a halt. Ahead of us glowed a very high door. I say "glowed," because that's exactly what it did. It was, like all else, a masterpiece of precious gems in pale colors.

"The Pearly Gates!" I whispered solemnly to Lydia. She giggled.

"Give it a rest; we've all been dead such a long time already, so we won't be needing any pearly gates to go through," she whispered back, with the same mock solemnity. "It's my guess that we are to see something special through there."

As usual, she was absolutely right. The lock squeaked a bit as the pearly gates opened up slowly. We kept closely behind our guide, but Lissa chose to walk through at Lydia's side.

We heard singing, at first only just audible, then increasingly stronger, with every step we took. Finally the sound was so powerful and so wonderfully beautiful that we just stood still. The closest comparison I can make would be with Negro spirituals, only in a stronger, purer form.

My greatest wish is that my readers may experience that which Lydia and I were so privileged to see on our travels, which is why I try to make Earthly comparisons, since I think it the best way, wouldn't you agree? This particular music had an ethereal clang that is somewhat difficult to convey, but similar tones have been successfully reproduced in certain operas such as Aida, parts of La belle Hélène or Orpheus in the Underworld, among others.

On Earth one totters out of the opera house into the rain pattering on the cobbles, the hubbub of traffic on the streets, or perhaps biting winter cold and sleet. Here we were not given quite such a rude awakening from our dreamy, musical experience. Having snuggled down into some of the comfortably upholstered chairs, which were positioned all over the place, we had either fallen asleep or into a sort of trance, which only felt gentle and pleasant to awaken from.

The Pilgrim stood, leaned over me, and patted me lightly on the shoulder, just as the final tones reverberated in the air like the breathing of Angels. I stumbled around, only half awake.

"Where are we?" I asked, rubbing my eyes.

"Just about the closest you can get to one of your opera houses!" exclaimed the grinning Pilgrim. "We call it the Palladium, as in your Rome. It is the stronghold of music in this part of Agartha. Some of what you heard was singing, but our singing sounds more like music being played, wouldn't you agree? We have other sorts, too, like the equivalent of your nursery rhymes and arias to operettas and musicals. The dolphins' song was included in what you heard – they are fantastic singers. All children are lulled into music right from birth; consequently, you will not find a single person here who is not musical. Furthermore, we have the elves' contribution to the musical part of Agartha; they are happy to perform at the Palladium, too."

"Do elves live here?" exclaimed Lydia and I, in surprised unison.

The Pilgrim nodded with a broad grin. "I thought we would visit them, too," he said.

I looked around the huge concert hall, still spellbound by the music that continued, barely audible to our ears. The inside, just like the exterior, glowed with jewels and beautiful paintings. The latter did not depict any religious motifs; they were mainly pictures of beings dancing and singing in groups. The walls appeared to be alive, for even though the pictures weren't compact, they had a singular way of softly moving very gently.

"Everything is in motion here. Beauty and motion held in elegance. Music and motion held in elegance. It is good for the soul. It imparts joy and enlightenment. Many come here purely to provide their souls with the nourishment they yearn, that is so desperately lacking on the surface. They do have pictures up there, of course, and some are beautiful, but the most typical contemporary ones represent only a sordid imagination. Human beings – as you also once were – devote themselves to the negative, that which we never speak of here in the Inner Earth. So similar and yet so very different."

He took out his whistle-pipe and blew it. It didn't take many seconds before the hovercraft materialized before us and we climbed up into it.

6. From the Old Fortress to Shamballa

"Most of the time I just wander around, but today I've made an exception," said the Pilgrim, as our vehicle rose up into the sky. "We are to travel quite a long distance, and this is the quickest way, since you wish to see some of the landscape."

The hovercraft came down lower, so that we cruised only a few feet above a meadow in bloom, which again reminded me of the prolific floral meadows of my childhood. I didn't have time to see in detail what was growing there, but I managed to glimpse some wild rose bushes bearing big, pink-colored flowers, much larger than ours usually are. The enlarged size of things, incidentally, seemed to generally apply to almost everything in this part of the world. Oxeye daisies, poppies, clover, and Timothy-grass appeared to have grown gigantic, and besides their new oversized form they'd even developed new colors. However, the forests were much like our Swedish ones, even if some of the varieties of trees could have been Mediterranean. There were various waterways, e.g., lakes, rivers, brooks, and streams; they gushed and gurgled along all over the place, and the wildlife looked lively. I glimpsed a number of deer, wolves, lynx, and ponderous bears easily making their way through the hilly terrain. I didn't see a single animal preying upon other animals.

"Surely the law of the jungle – to prey or be preyed upon – also applies here?" I asked our guide.

"No animals feast here," replied the Pilgrim. "All help themselves to the necessary fodder, but the type of slaughter practiced on the surface does not exist. Humans are not attacked, as long as they themselves do not attack, which is extremely rare. If it ever does happen, it's at the hand of Earthlings from above who have wandered astray. We're now about to land!"

The hovercraft dived rather abruptly into the jumble of trees and bushes. For a split second my heart jumped with fright, but the landing in itself was actually both soft and gently comfortable, despite the swift dive down. When I finally dared look up, I noticed that Lydia was doing the same, and I was somewhat surprised.

Ahead of us stood a fairy-tale castle. We saw it a little way off, since it was surrounded by a moat, just as fortresses always used to be built. There were at least two bridges we saw leading over to it. There was an abundance of turrets and towers, gleaming and shimmering with windows, vaults, and arches. It looked exactly like a picture from the thirteenth century.

"Yes, it is indeed a real fortress." The Pilgrim laughed when he saw our astonished looks. "This castle is truly ancient, from an age long before your concept of time, and it once existed on the surface. It belongs to an era when building was a noble art, and it was built with stones that cost the blood and sweat of many a poor peasant. It is an outstanding specimen of its kind, so when it started to crumble into ruin, during a dark age on Earth, we transported it here and set it up in a spot within our realm where we could restore it and keep it properly maintained. Dragons have assisted; some still remain within its close vicinity. Within its walls we have a research center – never revealed to humans – where our most eminent inventions and discoveries are developed. There's plenty of room, as you can imagine. Many superior minds are at work there; researchers who have lived part of their lives on Earth and have later been moved here."

"For example: Darwin, Tesla ..." I suggested. The Pilgrim nodded.

"They have peace and quiet here, and may communicate with one another if they wish. They have a magnificent park on the other side of the fortress, where they can wander around and ponder, with the added advantage of being able to enjoy refreshments, etc. The fortress is a tremendous facility, but regrettably I am unable to let you go in there, even if you aren't human beings from Earth. Currently an organization is being set up to receive and take care of Earth humans when the great changes occur that soon will take place on the surface of Earth. When this happens, all human beings will be forced to leave their homes for a time, since the Earth will have to be purified and reconstructed in order for it to be habitable again. Those who do not wish to leave the surface of the Earth will have to cross over in another way."

"You mean they will die?" retorted Lydia.

"Yes," acceded the Pilgrim mournfully. "There are people who can never change, who would rather perish in chaos and catastrophe than move here or to some other planet. Others will flee to our ships, where they will immediately be met with Love and joy, and be given the chance to improve the physical condition of their bodies. Healers and counselors to help will be legion."

We wandered around for a while and scrutinized the fortress from every possible angle, in order to permanently imprint it in our minds. We saw the glimmering, scaly dragons, every once in a while puffing out steam and glow. We even saw that some people, who had come out from within the castle, mounted the dragons and flew off.

"They are dragon-riders," explained the Pilgrim. "They are trained right from infancy to belong to one dragon and fly with it. Perhaps a seemingly daring enterprise, but many adventurous youths derive enormous pleasure from their uncommon mode of air travel. Now I must kindly ask that you re-embark the hovercraft standing over there. I can't promise it'll be a dragon-ride exactly, but perhaps quite exciting, anyway."

The air was just as warm as before, and I enjoyed the gentle breeze that caressed my face as we rose up into the air. The hovercraft did not fly quite as high or fast this time. As we left the fortress behind, seeing it become smaller and smaller in the distance, it felt as though we had all been part of an ancient saga, and I reveled in the thought. So, too, did Lydia, happily sitting with Lissa's head in her lap. The Pilgrim had resigned himself to his dog having turned to its newly devoted "mistress"; he just looked at the two of them together and smirked.

"I thought I might show you how this country is governed," announced the Pilgrim. "I presume this would interest both the pair of you and your readers. You should at least get some idea of how it works, since it's a perfect example of how the surface ought to be governed, and we sincerely hope it will be put into practice there as soon as possible. All your countries – and there are many – are governed differently. As a result, conflict and war constantly arise. There are two dimensions in existence here. In Telos, the town one arrives at if coming here via Mount Shasta, many three-dimensional human beings still live. This we can interpret as the town largely being physical, in your eyes."

"But we aren't physical," I protested. "I write through a physical medium, but Lydia and I are from an entirely different dimension and are to be counted as five-dimensional. We have ceased counting in dimensions; that is only for humans on Earth to adhere to. On Earth it is the physical that is of prime importance, which is why it is on the verge of destruction. Tangible riches, coupled with hate, envy, jealousy, and other despicable vices, are what rule the Earth. However, soon changes will come about, causing the Earth to return to its pristine, beautiful, flourishing state."

"And now we must truly forget the existence of the physical, apart from in Nature," declared the Pilgrim as the hovercraft descended. We had once again landed deep in the countryside, in a spot where the breathtakingly beautiful landscape was so flawless that Lydia and I were awed by it.

Similar countryside may also be found in various places on Earth – in Italy, for example. However, this particular spot appeared to encompass everything: the luxuriant vegetation combined with glittering waves from a small waterfall into a broad stream, the low murmuring pine trees in a little part of Swedish Dalecalian forest, multi-colored birds singing with joy while flying over the area and joined in with the singing and dancing that surrounded us.

This must certainly be the refuge of the Elementals, I mused. It was at that very moment I saw them! There were Elementals like fairies, elves, and many others all over the place; they danced, sang, and played strange instruments. They were of varying sizes, but all were extremely slender, almost transparent. Squirrels played among the tree trunks, while foxes and wolf cubs scampered, like clumsy babies, over the deep green moss at the edge of the wood. It's difficult to recount in detail this overwhelming mass, this bounteously abundant Nature.

"You simply must meet the Elementals before we move on to meet those governing here," beamed the Pilgrim, hustling us towards a high rock that was completely covered with luminous, emerald-green moss. The rock had an opening on one side that was the height of a man. Around the opening were carved and polished images; there were various animal heads, but also fauns and human heads with small horns. We didn't manage to see everything before the Pilgrim beckoned us to follow him and Lissa. We walked straight through the stone entrance.

Once inside, the entrance expanded into an enormous chamber, crowded with people. The Pilgrim walked through with both hands outstretched – everyone wanted to greet him. Since no one took any notice of us, we tried our utmost to register as much of the atmosphere, furnishings, and inhabitants there as we possibly could. This was no easy task, as the beings in there were constantly shoving and pushing, in order to reach our friend. I had earlier come across fairies, elves, dwarfs, little people and other Elementals on our travels, but nothing that ever quite matched this collection before. It was like entering a fairy-tale grotto.

"You are in the midst of an area where a great many Elementals reside," called out the Pilgrim, as he politely but determinedly drove away the swarms of them on and about him. "They usually make themselves invisible, blending in with Nature, to enable themselves to work in peace, but sometimes one is lucky enough to see them there, too. I wanted to show you how they live. This rock we've entered is an excellent example, although a little over-populated just at the moment, I think!"

Gradually we managed to back out, and now the Elementals at last made way for us to pass. The chamber was huge, and exquisitely adorned with both flowers and intricately made objects, chiefly out of precious stones. There were several tables with stools around them, and light shone through a hole in the roof, which radiated warm rays that danced down in shimmering cascades of light.

The Pilgrim and Lissa led the way for us out of the rock chamber. When we came back out to the stream with the waterfall, pale undines (water spirits) were dancing in the middle of it, as giddy and boisterous as the water's own playfulness. We hurried back to the hovercraft and were soon back up in the air.

"I wanted you to see how the Elementals co-operate with the Agarthans, even in their council. We shall now head for the capital city of Shamballa," proclaimed the Pilgrim. "If you hadn't first taken a glimpse of the natural habitat of the Elementals, it would have made it decidedly more difficult for you to follow the council discussions. We are about to enter an entirely five-dimensional zone, but it won't affect you, since you're in fact already there. We shall just make a few small adjustments to your structure, to enable you to be in your natural state. You are far too physically embodied and human-like at the moment."

I actually felt a metamorphosis in my body and noticed that Lydia, too, was reacting. We became a little disoriented; our heads felt giddy and I thought I would faint, but the dizziness swiftly passed. When I looked at my hand, it didn't look as firm and sinewy as in its physical state, but much thinner. Lydia's handsome profile next to me had taken an unreal look about it – a sort of pale, soft shimmer. We had become Angels again!

The hovercraft didn't land on the ground this time; instead it positioned itself gently and carefully on a balustrade, or perhaps part of the roof. It actually looked rather like a roof, even if such things were rather unusual in this land. The roof was domed, reaching about six feet up to the ceiling, with a wide surrounding balcony. The dome looked like it was made of gold and had a great hole in the center, enabling either the sun to shine in or the night moon to gently rock the stars to sleep to the faint sound of harmonious music that came from somewhere within.

"There's an entrance this way," explained the Pilgrim and led us to a shiny, golden, embellished door. He opened it, revealing that the balcony, or roof terrace, continued through it, a couple of floors up from the circular room below. This type of domed architecture is known as a day-lighting cupola, or roof lantern.

When we leaned over the solid golden bannister, we could see down into the great chamber below. Naturally the chamber was circular, and was adorned with the most fantastic collection of paintings and sculptures. A long table with twelve chairs along it was laid with gold brocade and sparkling goblets. All but one chair was occupied by powerful, humanlike figures, the exception being an almost transparent entity, sitting on the chair closest to one end – most probably an elf. At the head of each end sat two very imposing personages – a man at one end and a woman at the other. The Pilgrim beckoned to us.

"There's a stairway over here; follow me," he whispered, and we fell in behind him. It was a white spiral staircase that appeared to be made of marble – incredibly well made, with an ornate bannister winding downwards. Lydia stopped still behind me. The Pilgrim had already reached the chamber below and was waiting for us.

"I dare not," whispered Lydia, her body shaking all over.

"Dare not what?" I hissed with annoyance. "If you are afraid to go down, then take hold of my hand." I climbed back up a few steps. "I have to admit that the staircase is pretty steep."

Lydia stood frozen to the spot, still shaking, even though she had put her hand into mine. I could sense that something was dreadfully wrong.

"It feels like appearing before God!" Lydia was white as a sheet, and her hand was shaking uncontrollably in mine. "It isn't only the staircase that terrifies me; it's also the gang waiting down there."

I went back another step and managed to grab hold of her waist and lift her close to me. "Now I'm transferring some of my security to you," I coaxed, and carried her light weight down the stairs.

At the bottom the Pilgrim smilingly waited for us, together with a woman. She was a tall, upright woman, with golden-blonde hair that reached her shoulders. She was extremely beautiful. She wore a long, white dress embroidered with gold and with a wide, gold belt. I noticed that one chair in the middle of the long table stood unoccupied.

"My name is Helena," she said, taking hold of both of Lydia's hands while I put my Angel friend down on the floor. She then put her arms around Lydia and gave her a hug and a warm, friendly smile, saying, "I am the commander of an Alpha ship and I am here to receive information concerning the imminent great changes that will happen on Earth. At that moment, the entire Space fleet with its millions of spaceships must be on the alert, you see. But right now, all I see is a frightened little girl whom I want to help and comfort."

Tears ran down Lydia's cheeks. "Silly me," she sniveled. "I know how kind you all are, but it seemed so very ceremonious here that it brought me to a point of trepidation."

Helena burst into laughter. "This must be just about the least dangerous place you could possibly be!" she exclaimed. "I shall now introduce you to all my friends at the table." She took out her lace-edged handkerchief to dry Lydia's eyes with, and patted her soothingly until she went into a fit of laughter. Beautiful Helena was a lovely person; the description "golden girl" did not perhaps perfectly fit this exquisite being, but the implication was correct. "Heaven's golden girl," I thought to myself, inwardly smiling. I have learned to adopt the inward smile when in distinguished company.

7. The Distinguished Society Governing Agartha

Now I, Jan, would like to make clear to my readers that I am not at liberty to give the names of each and every individual seated at the golden table. A few have given me permission to reveal their names; others have not. However, I can certainly promise that this gathering of wise men and women truly exists in Agartha, working very hard to give help to the Earth in the best possible way. Helena has no objection to having her name revealed; Mariana has physically seen her and furthermore communicated with her psychically. Helena has herself given her account of her first meeting with Lydia and we have heartily laughed about the petite, petrified Angel.

Helena led Lydia straight to the transparent entity that sat closest to us. He (for, despite his translucence, somehow he gave a masculine impression) politely stood up and gallantly kissed both of Lydia's hands with butterfly kisses. To me he cast a cheerful smile and an amicable nod.

"I am Alric," he announced, in a voice with a surprisingly high-pitched ring to it. "I represent the elf kingdom, which I know you previously are acquainted with. Welcome to Shamballa, the Pearl of Wisdom!"

The whole time Helena led Lydia by the hand while I traipsed along behind with the Pilgrim and Lissa, who seemed completely at home in these divine circles. The next Master was Hilarion; I knew him from before – a jovial and pleasant man. They were all very tall, but especially him. He was thin, sinewy, and a little stooped, but then he straightened himself up and his deep blue eyes flashed piercingly.

"Well if it isn't Jan!" he exclaimed. "My dear old friend! How are you keeping these days?" He stretched out his long arms and gave me a big hug. "You have a beautiful girl with you, I see! Watch out for Janne, little girl; he is wild and dangerous!" Then he heaved with laughter and indicated to us to move along. "Off you go now – Kuthumi next!"

Kuthumi I also recognized, although not quite as well as Hilarion. Kuthumi had helped spread theosophy on Earth, but humans had not yet been ready to accept this wisdom. He was currently working together with the other Masters, preparing for the imminent salvation and metamorphosis of the Earth.

All of a sudden we were hit by a violent blast of wind, right between two chairs. I immediately sensed who was playing the joke on me; he is a very dear friend of mine – always getting up to pranks. After hearing a few joyous tones on a panpipe I caught sight of Peter Pan, the God of Nature, boisterously crashing down from his chair to give me an enormous great bear hug.

"What a stroke of luck that I happened to be here today!" he boomed with his warm, powerful voice. "We have an important meeting concerning the Earth and I must therefore participate, since my entire world of flora and fauna is about to change – hopefully for the better! The Earth will flourish as never before. It will become the most beautiful planet in our entire Universe, as was intended from the beginning – and humankind will be its most devoted servant!"

"I thought humankind would become free in light and joy – not forgetting Love!" I responded.

"Service is not to be confused with servitude," retorted Pan. "Humankind must recognize the connection between both flora and fauna, which entails a brotherhood-sisterhood wherein all life is respected and cared for. We shall dare show ourselves to human beings, without fear of intimidation or maltreatment from them."

"Oh you wonderful, free world!" I exclaimed. "May you soon conquer the minds of humankind and transform them into diligent pupils in the school of life. Regrettably, we can see the evening newspapers' shocking news from our protected dimension, whether we wish and intend to try to do something about this. We are fighting against dark forces, Pan, and I sincerely hope that we shall triumph!"

We hugged one another, and Pan even embraced Lydia. I noticed her pensive expression. An Angel finding herself in the arms of a fur-clad man with a goat's horn is probably more than a little unusual. However, we continued on to the next chair where, once again, a very good friend sat; namely, the Master and Count of Saint Germain. We went literally from one embrace into another, and I observed that even our friend the Pilgrim did likewise. Lissa trotted along, proudly holding her head and tail up high, graciously accepting all the friendly little pats she received. Then Pan did a little waltz with the Pilgrim's dog, just as though she was a charming dancing partner.

"My dear Jan, who would ever have thought I'd meet you here!" Saint Germain beamed with pleasure at me. As I spotted the Pilgrim also happily greeting him as an old friend, my suspicions as to whether the twain might be one and the same man were dispelled. Nay, the Pilgrim was quite a different Master, whose integrity was not to be negated or tainted. The Count of Saint Germain – also called Prince Ragoczy – was a magnificent manifestation. His splendid, burgundy-colored mantle was clasped together at the neck with a seven-pointed gold star, studded with diamonds, amethysts, and emeralds. One could so easily have concluded that a mere eighteenth-century fop stood before one, but the moment the Count started to speak, any such superficial assumptions instantly vanished. Furthermore, he exuded such overwhelming charisma that his entire being appeared to be haloed in light.

"He is the Master of the Seventh Ray," I must have thought aloud, since Lydia then asked, "What do you mean by the Seventh Ray, Jan? What are these rays you speak of?"

I was forced to answer this, because it occurred to me that neither are my readers likely to be acquainted with the Ray system of the Masters in the Great White Brotherhood. A cursory glance around the table revealed that the Planetary Hierarchy was represented and its seven Masters were present. All that remained was to try to explain this to our confused little Angel, Lydia. The Pilgrim saw my hesitation and gave vent to a good-humored laugh.

"If you won't tell Lydia, then I will!" he teased. We had arrived at the short end of the long table.

I nodded my grateful assent, "Please do!"

"We have just come to the Master of the First Ray, El Morya," the Pilgrim explained. We stood at the foot of the podium upon which the table was standing, so our voices were rather difficult to hear, since we were speaking quietly, almost telepathically, to one other. "El Morya originally comes from the planet Mercury, and he is considered to be the representative of God's Will. He works fervently for the Earth's liberation from the dark forces and for transformation to represent the Light and Love. Here we have a strictly and strategically educated man, whose competence is urgently needed on Earth.

"The Master of the Second Ray is called Lanto. He is of Chinese origin. Specifically unique to Lanto is that the light from his heart is visible in his body. He is very closely connected with Master Saint Germain; they often work together on various projects

"Ray number Three, known as the Ray of Love, is attributed to Paul the Venetian, who once incarnated as Paolo Veronese – a not exactly unknown painter in Italy, wouldn't you say? He was incarnated in Atlantis and managed to leave for Peru before the continent sank into the ocean. He represents not only humankind's Love and tolerance for one another, but also the beauty in art.

"Serapis Bey is the Master of the Fourth Ray. He guarantees the strict discipline, that which comes from within, so that one can express one's deepest Inner Self in the correct manner. It is said that he originates from Venus. One of the lives he has lived on Earth was as the famous Pharaoh Akhenaten. He still works for the Brotherhood in Luxor, together with the Seraphs.

"The Master of the Fifth Ray is Hilarion, whom we just met here a moment ago. He is here in the capacity of spokesman, representing all the Rays.

"At last we have a woman, Lady Nada, who is the Sixth Ray representative. She represents development of many civilizations and also for Divine Love, right from childhood. She actively involves herself in all animal and plant life, so of course she is well acquainted with Pan. Lady Nada is present; she is sitting over there."

He nodded in a direction diagonally across the table. There sat a fair-haired woman of slight build with enormous blue eyes, dressed in a shimmering pink frock and glittery shawl, bearing jewelry that looked like roses.

"Most attractive," whispered Lydia. "I should very much like to meet her."

"And so you shall, very soon," the Pilgrim whispered back. "We have only the Seventh Ray left, whom you've already a moment ago learned is the Count of Saint Germain — so now we can continue around the table, introducing ourselves to all those who wish to be greeted."

8. The Prophecies of the Hopi Indians

A signal sounded, which meant that someone wished to say something and demanded silence from all others present. A man at the far, short end of the table stood up. He raised both his arms and gently smiled at the gathering.

"I beg your attention!" he called out in his powerfully sonorous voice. "We have in our midst visitors from the Heavenly Spheres. Our noble friend, the Pilgrim, has brought with him a man and a woman. They have come here on a mission to later convey their impressions of Agartha to a higher dimension. As you know, I am Hilarion, and have been bestowed the happy task of warmly welcoming our honored guests in the way true to our tradition!"

At this point, happy laughter burst forth and friendly eyes focused upon us. The Pilgrim herded us up on the podium and I bowed in all directions, while Lydia gently smiled and nodded. The Pilgrim was evidently a person well known within the circle of Masters.

Wonderful music suddenly became audible, sweetly-scented aromas filled the air, and an invisible choir sang so beautifully, it compared with nothing I'd ever heard before. It all felt so magnificently magical. All this went on for quite some time until eventually the music and singing faded away, permitting Hilarion to continue speaking.

"I take it we all are well aware that the prophecies made by the Hopi Indians on the surface have already started taking place? They spoke of the Earth's change in 2012, i.e., their prophecies were valid only up until the end of that year. I would like to remind you of some parts which I consider urgent at present on the surface."

Lydia, the Pilgrim, and I had each been allotted a chair at the edge of one of the short ends of the table, so I understood this was to be a longer speech. Hilarion gently smiled at us and continued with his address.

"If we were to divide the world into cycles, the first would be the Mineral Kingdom, then the Plant Kingdom, then the Animal Kingdom, and after that it was intended that the Human Kingdom would follow. We have now come to the end of the Animal Kingdom cycle and have learned how to live as animals on Earth.

"In the beginning of our cycle, the Great Spirit came down to Earth and revealed himself. He gathered people together on an island – which now lies under the water and, as you know was Atlantis – and he then told them this: 'I shall send you four cardinal points and give you four skin tones. You are to gain knowledge that you will call the Ancient Wisdom. When you reconvene, you will impart your accumulated knowledge to one another and you shall become a great and wise civilization, living in peace. I will be presenting you with two stone tablets. These must absolutely not be dropped and let fall to the ground, for should this happen, the Earth will suffer and eventually die.'

"In this way we all were given the responsibility that we call our Guardianship. To the Red race he entrusted the Earth. They were to learn all about the plants that grow in the soil, the food we can eat, and the herbs we can use to heal with. This knowledge was to be shared with the others.

"The Yellow race was accorded responsibility for the Air. They were to learn all about air and breathing – how it may be utilized for spiritual development.

"To the Black race he bestowed stewardship of the Water. They were made to understand that water is the most humble, yet most powerful, of all the elements.

"Finally, the White race was given charge of the Fire. Fire consumes, but it is also motion. The White race should move across the face of the Earth in order to unite all the races as one human family. But all this has, regrettably, been forgotten. Only the Hopi Indians have hidden and kept the knowledge.

"The Hopis still have the two stone tablets of the Red race in

54

Arizona. The Black race keeps theirs in Kenya and the Yellow race keeps theirs in Tibet.

"The stone tablets of the White race are supposed to be in Switzerland, but they are never spoken of – they are a closed chapter. Perhaps they are still there, perhaps not.

"The Hopis have always retained the belief that the Earth will of its own accord be cleansed and rise again. To live in that age – that we all know is now – is both the hardest endurable lifetime, but also the most eminent. We are currently right in the middle of this purification, which many call the Apocalypse.

"Nostradamus predicted the great earthquakes on Earth. They have already started to occur. War raging in the east and several other places. Mankind giving vent to their desires under the shadow of evil. However, Love still remains, and we are many who safeguard it and spread it."

With this, Hilarion ended his speech, which was met with hearty applause, accompanied by the magnificent music that once again rang out all around us, seemingly coming from nowhere.

Lady Nada hurried up onto the podium before the music ceased. She stretched up both her arms to signal that she wished to speak. Hilarion remained standing behind her until the music ebbed away into an exquisitely resonant chord.

"I wish to speak for womankind!" Lady Nada cried out. Her voice was far more powerful than I had imagined.

"In the times imminently upon us, when the Earth is to undergo a complete metamorphosis, women will be needed more than ever before. I have no desire whatsoever to belittle the undertakings of men, but I would like to remind my fellow sisters that we must join all our forces if we are to cope with the distress, despair, hardship, and terror that is about to take place. Now all of us sisters are brimming to the hilt with healing power, energy, and empathy. Things we consider we may not do, or are unable to do, will be communicated to us via the Beings of Light, which each of you has the right to summon. Never forget that we are not alone; we all work together and are equals with varying experience and expertise to be exercised and divulged. We are all magical women, and pragmatically apply our magic where it is constantly needed. United, sisters, we are strong! As strong as Life itself!"

At this point the next deafening applause burst forth, accompanied by another heart-rending experience of music. Lady Nada moved towards Lydia and winked at her with a glint in her eye.

"Spread this message to all sisters in the glittering army of the stars!" she whispered, whereupon the two of them embraced each another warmly.

"It is now high time for us to leave," announced the Pilgrim, taking hold of my arm and Lydia's hand. He bowed courteously, and we followed suit. It fell completely silent in the chamber while we paraded out, closely followed by a beautiful dog with its tail up high, ready to set out on a new adventure.

Our faithful vehicle, the hovercraft, was still standing outside the building, waiting for us. I was still a bit stunned from all the ceremonious atmosphere we had left behind, so I simply clambered up and fell straight on top of Lissa, who understandingly and kindly snuffled my leg and licked my hand.

"Now we shall rest ourselves from all the ceremony, and pay a visit to the School of Dragon-Riders," proclaimed the Pilgrim, as we sailed up into the somewhat cooler, but still completely clear, air.

9. The Dragon-Riders

When the hovercraft was landing, we saw a fence, or some sort of grille, and a passage that we, presumably, were to go through. We heard a hard flapping noise and shortly afterwards saw its source. A man, who was uncommonly short for being an Agarthan, came running towards us. He wasn't a young man, but nevertheless appeared rather agile, muscular, and fit. He was gray-haired, with a short, pointed beard and laughing, bluish-gray eyes. He rushed up to the Pilgrim, embraced him, and then turned towards us. Lissa reacted as though she knew him well.

"My name is Sirq, and I am a dragon-rider," he introduced himself with a beaming smile. "I teach young ladies and gentlemen to become dragon-riders – and that is no easy task. Come with me and you will see what I mean."

We followed along after him, through a little woodland area, and behind the trees an opening shone through. We came to a gallery that clearly was made for spectators. It stood rather high, the reason for which soon became evident to us, once having painstakingly climbed up all the steps.

Before us was a stretch of grass, about the size of a football field, and below us was a grandstand for spectators. But that which was happening out in the field was the most fascinating thing I'd seen in a long time. As usual, Lydia squeezed my arm tightly whenever she was excited and in high spirits.

Lined up was a row of glittering dragons in varying tones of green. I counted seven of them. By each dragon was a busy young person who, despite their considerable height, looked like a little leprechaun against the mighty beasts overshadowing them. They were fully occupied washing the dragons' noses, showering them between their great scales, and cleaning their feet. Some of the dragons were lying down and obediently allowing themselves to be attended to, while others stood up, stamping impatiently and flapping and beating their wings.

"This is the School of Dragon-Riders," Sirq informed us. "We educate impressionists. The impressionists are those rare individuals who have found and grown up with their very own dragon egg, and consequently made an impression on the dragon-embryo developing inside. The twain are permanently bound to one another in an inextricably powerful way. I shall go down and ask one of the boys to fly with his dragon, so that you may see how it works."

"Perhaps you would like to test-ride a dragon?" the Pilgrim inquired. "If you don't quite dare, then I can accompany you. It's quite all right with two riders; I can fly with Jan, if Sirq will take care of Lydia."

All we had seen certainly gave us the urge to try it out. One of the dragons, that had been standing up, bent to lie down and enable its rider to climb up into the saddle. These great, solid saddles were attached to the dragons, much like camel saddles, only twice as large. Each dragon-rider positioned himself behind his own dragon's relatively small ears, so that speaking or giving orders would be clearly heard, maintaining good contact. The boy leaned forward and stroked the tip of the dragon's ear, which instigated its ascent into the air. Breathlessly, we gazed at how the great beast so softly and elegantly rose into the sky and flew a little while in circles around us. Then the dragon started to dive down, go around, and ascend again.

"He's looping," shrieked Lydia, and the Pilgrim nodded. "This is incredible! Do you dare to ride, Janne?" I nodded, but inside I wasn't quite so sure. Certainly, I had ridden many times throughout my journeys, but never quite such an enormous animal. Unless flying machines can be perceived as dragons, of course? I smirked at the very thought.

The demonstration in the air was over. Sirq had returned to the gallery. "Would you care for a little ride, my friends?" he asked. "There are two very kind old dragons who are used to tourists. Their impressionists will accompany you and, if you wish, so too will the Pilgrim and I, in which case, someone will have to look after Lissa, for she becomes fretful when her master goes dragon riding. She's seen it many times before. We could, of course, tie her on very tightly, if you'd prefer to take her with you, Pilgrim. But in that case, there will definitely be no looping, that I can promise!"

He led us down from the gallery and Lissa started to whimper. I almost felt like doing so myself, for the terrifyingly huge beasts scared me a bit. An Angel must not be frightened, and I averted my gaze from Lydia, who was walking arm in arm with Sirq while the Pilgrim bound his dog.

One could actually see that the two dragons we had been led to were elderly. They had not been lined up from the beginning, and the young dragons appeared to act most reverently towards them. They stood elegantly and bowed their heads repeatedly at the enormous newcomers. I felt trapped, with no chance of escape. I watched while Lydia went up to one of the old dragons, patted it on the nose, and whispered something in its rather large, "little" ear. The dragon actually answered by snorting out a few little puffs of smoke from its nostrils and drawing its big upper lip up into a sort of smile.

Sirq helped her up and jumped up behind her. Her dragon was fitted with a double-saddle that really looked quite comfortable; mine had one the same. I did as Lydia had done; I went up and patted my dragon's enormous nose and received a contented puff of smoke in return. The Pilgrim sat behind me, and upon both dragons sat also an impressionist. I rather think that the dragons only obeyed orders from their impressionists, so we waited for an announcement for take-off. It came!

The sensation could be felt in my stomach, despite it being an Angel's one. I was not perfectly clear about how human-like I really was at this stage, since the Agarthans were special, if one compared them with ordinary humans on the surface. So I simply had to resign myself to the fact that my Angel stomach tied itself in knots just a little when we soared up into the sky. The hovercraft sometimes floated up pretty high, too, but that was more like being in a helicopter. There was nothing helicopter-like about the dragon I was bound tightly to.

Lydia's dragon stayed pretty well parallel with mine to begin with, but then all of a sudden shot off at great speed.

The sky was completely cloudless, and Agartha's sun, that I knew to be artificial and extremely pleasant, drew closer without it becoming hotter. I delighted in sitting there with the Pilgrim's hands secured around my waist. Lissa was just behind her master; she, too, was well secured with rope. He had decided to allow his dog to feel how it was to sit on a dragon, which Lissa seemed to understand, and without struggling she had let herself be tied to the saddle. I had read books about dragon-riders when I lived on Earth and had never thought it particularly remarkable. As far as I was concerned, dragons had always existed in reality, although I never dared write about them. But I certainly told stories of dragons to my children when they were small, although the ones I told of were probably not such kindly dragons as these.

I heard a scream, or rather more of a wail, and saw Lydia's dragon far ahead of mine. It was flying askew, as if it was about to topple. Lydia looked as though she had come loose from Sirq's grip.

"We must go to them; something has happened!" exclaimed the Pilgrim, and he gave an order to the apprentice-rider who, in turn, immediately whispered into our dragon's ear. It subsequently took a swift dive and flew at such high speed to the other dragon that, before I even had time to think, we were underneath it and saw Lydia with the top half of her body hanging out of the saddle. Sirq had a firm grip around her waist.

"I'll transfer her over via teleportation," he yelled. "Our dragon is ill and must be taken home. I'll stay here."

In a jiffy, Lydia was in front of me in the saddle, while our dragon hovered in the air. Quick as lightning, the Pilgrim bound a shimmering rope around her, so that she was firmly fixed. I looked at her deathly-pale face and whispered, "Keep calm, my Angel. You are in safe hands now, and we are returning to the ground."

"He looped, even though he wasn't allowed to," she weakly

responded, and presumably fainted, for she fell backwards with her head against my shoulder.

"We'll soon be back on the ground," comforted the Pilgrim, and our dragon spread out its wings and sailed as fast as the wind, though safely and soundly, straight down to the dragon runway. Finally on terra firma, I at last took a deep breath while we jointly helped untie Lydia and laid her down on a bench in the gallery. Lissa bounded up to her and started eagerly sniffing and licking her all over.

"Take the dog away," I snapped at the Pilgrim.

He laughed out loud. "No," he patiently replied, "because Lissa is healing her. Lissa is a healing-dog. When Lydia awakens, she will remember nothing of the accident, but will just think she's returned from a wonderful flying trip – so lovely, in fact, that she just dozed off. It is best so."

Well, well – a dog that's an authentic healer, indeed! Lissa was undoubtedly a very fine dog, but I'd never have suspected that dogs had the ability to cure people – just the reverse! Henceforth I shall have to regard these fantastic animals quite differently. But I had learned a great deal more about animals that day. The dragons also were absolutely fantastic.

As though he had just read my mind, the Pilgrim then said, "It is possible to converse with dragons. There really are dragons that can speak, although mostly telepathically. Their level of intelligence can be compared with that of the dolphins – and a dolphin's intellect is higher than a human's. You will hear more about this on Sirius. Sadly, Lydia's dragon must have been taken ill, which very rarely happens. You had a stroke of extremely bad luck. Occasionally dragons manage to catch and eat something that doesn't agree with them while flying."

"However, first we have to go to the Pleiades, to visit a planet there," I said, "although right now I would prefer to stay a while longer in Agartha. There is so very much to see and learn here."

"You and Lydia are welcome to come home with me to my dwelling, so that I can answer any questions you may have and tell you a little more about the country you now find yourself in."

His dwelling? I thought the Pilgrim was an eternally wandering soul. He must have spotted what I was thinking, for in that very instant he laughed out loud and patted me on the shoulder.

"I certainly do wander around a great deal," he remarked, "but I also intermittently return home and rest a while, partly because Lissa also needs to relax now and then. She means everything to me. There are a few things you've yet to find out about Agartha – for example, how it is governed and why it seems so peaceful and harmonious here. The hovercraft awaits us!"

10. Crystal Cities and Clan System

The hovercraft was a magical vehicle. Lydia didn't seem the least bit interested in what had happened while she had slept, but just jumped up into the hovercraft with a radiantly happy face.

"So good that we're to find out how Agartha is run!" she exclaimed. "I am so terribly curious to know. I know we met the twelve in that beautiful building, but I still don't fully understand how everything works here. How is it possible for things to be so calm and well organized, and all the people so happy, too? Even the animals seem so wise, and not in the least aggressive. I haven't heard a single dog bark since we arrived here, but all the more birdsong – almost too much sometimes." She laughed and blew kisses to unseen birds, hiding in the trees.

We were all the more bewildered, after arriving at the Pilgrim's dwelling. It was a cave in the woods, deeply embedded in greenery growing all over the place, making it virtually impossible to detect, had it not been for certain special markings he'd made by the woodland path we walked along. It was strange enough just stepping out of the hovercraft in the middle of a wood, but then Lissa actually started barking joyful little "woofs" and simultaneously waving her tail up high. Soon, however, we couldn't even see her erect tail, as we followed after our friend, deep into a primeval forest.

The entrance to the cave was sealed by a door, which swung wide open as we arrived. Dumbfounded, we stepped over the tree-trunk threshold and came directly into a cozy room with stone walls and a stone floor, and an open fireplace that blazed warmly. Facing the fire stood a long, curved sofa and a coffee table. The Pilgrim invited us to sit down. In an instant a tray appeared, laden with mouth-wateringly aromatic sandwiches and a jug of delicious Agarthan beer. We were ravenous at that point, and even Lydia partook of the feast with good appetite. When we had quelled our hunger, the Pilgrim started to speak.

"One cannot concentrate so well on an empty stomach," he said, laughing. "You wished to know how Agartha is governed, so I shall explain as though you were human beings from the surface – as you actually have been!

"That the Earth is hollow, you already know. Your leaders have throughout the centuries succeeded in withholding this fact, for fear of it leading to their own diminished power over Mother Earth. It could even – oh woe! – lead to improvements within society and other, better, ways of thinking being put into practice, the consequences of which might prove disastrous for those in positions of power.

"One might say that the Earth has an inner crust that is the continuation of the outer one. At both poles there are entrances in the form of holes, where the crust folds itself downwards and slips into the cavity therein. Inside this cavity is where the tunnels begin. The outer and inner crusts have a similar topography: both are comprised of seas, continents, mountains, lakes, and rivers. The core of the inner part, i.e., the Central Sun, is enveloped by a veil of cloud. The light thence is weaker than the outer Sun's, so that daylight in the Inner Earth is softer than on the outer. Inside the Inner Earth there are so-called Cavern worlds. These are enormous holes, many of which have been created naturally by Mother Earth, while others have been constructed by applying advanced Agarthan technology. This land is the very last surviving part of Lemuria."

"Does that mean we're really sitting in Lemuria right now?" interjected Lydia, somewhat startled.

"In a way – yes!" replied the Pilgrim, smiling. "And also in Atlantis, if you like. But the Atlantis leaders were not kind to the Lemurians. They sealed up all the entrances to Lemuria – that is to say, present day Agartha. Just prior to the destruction of Atlantis, the Lemurians managed to break the seals, thereby saving many surface human beings from certain death. Unfortunately, Anunnaki instead became rulers of the surface, and I know you've heard how it ended up with them." *(Mariana's comment: I have written about that in my previously released book on Agartha.)*

I nodded.

"Very good. It's not a very pleasant chapter to talk about." The Pilgrim served us some more refreshments. Lissa crept up close to Lydia and looked as though she was listening intently to her master.

"The Lemurians who survived the Great Flood gathered together and named their new community Agartha. The capital city, Shamballa, began being built in a cavern that lay far down beneath the town of Lhasa, in what still is Tibet on the surface. Still today there are many tunnels running between Shamballa and the upper part of the Himalayas. These were used by holy men who sought out the surface world in order to spread their wisdom and are still doing so, although with less success, since there are fewer who listen.

"Agartha's world is really rather similar to the surface world. The Inner Earth encompasses a flourishing ecosystem where you can re-discover animals and plants that have become extinct on the surface. Agartha's inhabitants take care of and preserve this fauna and flora. The Agarthans themselves live in crystal cities that are dotted around the entire Inner Earth.

"Agartha has, over a period of time, created a sort of living, Galactic Society. A system of twelve clans exists at the heart of their society. These clans are organized in accordance with their respective assignments – for example: administration, technology, healing, research, etc. Each clan consists of a number of pods, which in turn consists of a number of podlets. It is common practice for podlets and pods from one clan to communicate with the others in the other eleven clans. The pods and podlets form mini communities, each of which has sufficient resources to creatively find solutions to any eventual problems that may arise.

"The Governing Council of Agartha consists of twelve principal members from the clans. These have been chosen on account of the services they have provided for the clans and the society. The Governing Council selects an individual deemed as the wisest. This person is bestowed the title of King or Queen and is given the responsibility for an immense army of emissaries or liaison officers who are sent to the world above and to the Galactic Federation Council.

"An advanced form of technology called replicators enables every person to themselves create their own daily food and clothing. Each crystal city is consequently independent, since neither building construction, agriculture, nor any other form of manufacturing occurs. Everyone individually creates their own way of life in the way that suits them. Technology also manages to transport people anywhere in an instant…"

"In other words, hovercrafts are really superfluous," pronounced Lydia, who thought this was a good moment to cut in.

"You ought to know," responded the Pilgrim, smiling, "that this superb technology at this very moment is utilized in an attempt to unite Agartha with her surface brothers and sisters. Even for us, it is fun and enriching to be able to study Nature from a hovercraft. We are furthermore delighted to have the opportunity of sharing our knowledge." At this point he fell silent and we all heartily clapped our hands until Lissa started to growl. She thought we were rather rowdy, I assume.

"Have a little rest here now, before we fly onwards!" suggested the Pilgrim. Lydia gratefully laid her head on a cushion on the sofa and pulled her legs up around her. Lissa snoozed, closely snuggled up next to her. I looked questioningly at the Pilgrim and he beckoned to me.

"Would you like to learn more before you leave us?" he inquired, and I raced after his flapping cowl. I caught up with him at the hovercraft, ready for yet another spacewalk.

"We haven't spoken very much about Telos, or even visited it, other than the fleeting arrival welcome you and Lydia received at Boron's. The town is built in five levels, which is perhaps a little difficult to comprehend for a former surface dweller."

"Not at all," I earnestly responded. "My wife took great pride in baking cake in several layers, and so this is nothing new to me. What a fascinating idea, to build a town up in tiers."

"It's ingenious in many ways," replied the Pilgrim. "Deep down and high up, you see! Highest up, if we start at the top, you have the center for trade and administration. It's positioned quite close to the surface. The upper part is pyramid-shaped. This is where all the public and official buildings are, including a big hotel for visitors from the surface. Also situated there are a communication tower, an airfield, and miscellaneous residences."

"Trade?" I interjected. "An airfield for spacecraft? Why does the surface know nothing about this?"

"Telos is situated close to the surface and is slightly influenced by the human beings on the surface," said the Pilgrim, grinning. "On level four, there are residential areas, and fabrication using no machinery. All the houses are round and there are dwellings for single people, couples, and larger families. Since the houses are circular, they never become dusty – something overlooked by those on Earth!

"There is organic farming on the third level. Our environmentally friendly cultivation is extremely advanced. Fruit, vegetables, and soya products are twice as tasty and prolific as those grown on the surface. Solely vegetarian food can be found here.

"On level two there is more agriculture, some manufacturing, and some parks.

"The first level is Nature's. All the animals that have become extinct on the surface can be found there, and a different fauna, too. Violence and killing is absent."

"How do they manage to survive?" I marveled.

"Nature must take its course. People do not kill the animals and vice versa, since the animals do not see them as their enemy. Some species we feed, as in a zoo. Some become ill, and the young can lose their parents, but we see to it that all is taken care of and set on its right course. There are a great many people working with animals and plants."

While the Pilgrim talked, we travelled around, popping up and down like golf balls. We didn't stop anywhere, but I saw more species of animals than I'd ever encountered during my Earthly life. But then I started to become anxious about Lydia.

"She would never have managed to take all this," remarked the Pilgrim. "You will have to tell her all about it during your continued journey."

"I have another question," I announced. "Do you all speak the same language throughout the whole country?"

"We speak a tongue we call the sun-language, but the dialects vary from one town to another. We have a highly advanced computer system, which everyone uses."

"You have computers?" I exclaimed delightedly. "How come I haven't seen any?"

"Because they don't look like the ones on the surface," came the answer, and I again caught a mischievous boyish glint in my friend's eye. "And they work a lot better, without a mass of leads and hassle. Furthermore, they cost nothing, for money isn't used here. Good, eh?"

"Then you can't go to the cinema or theater?" I admonished.

The Pilgrim slapped me on the shoulder. "But of course we can!" he retorted. "There's an abundance of such entertainment here. How do you otherwise imagine we should be able to learn anything? We have Porthologos, which has a great deal to offer, but there are many other entertainment centers, too. All one has to do is go there; no tickets are necessary."

The hovercraft slowed down and swayed above the moss in the woodland, just outside the Pilgrim's home. Inside we found a somewhat irate Lydia, who had just woken up, so the reception was rather like a good ticking off. But the Pilgrim just laughed it off and served up a most delicious vegetarian dish and some Agarthan wine, to build up our strength in preparation for our departure to the Pleiades. It really was a tremendous undertaking!

11. Next: Pleiades

"Who are you, really?" I asked the Pilgrim, once we had concluded the most exquisite farewell meal in his cave.

He responded with an indefinable smile and gravely replied, "That is a question I might perhaps answer when we meet again. I am hoping you will return to Agartha before you finally embark on your journey home. Otherwise Lissa will be most upset – and so shall I!"

Lydia threw her arms around the neck of the somewhat startled Pilgrim and gave him a couple of great smacking kisses on both his cheeks.

"You can count on it!" she promised. "Both Janne and I absolutely love it here – and next time I want to be guided around Telos. Besides which, I would dearly love to see Boron, Tulli, and Nelsea again. Please do give them our love, won't you?"

The Pilgrim nodded emphatically and his beautiful dog, Lissa, sat with sadly bowed head; she would miss Lydia.

"If you should find you are in desperate need of help, then you may call for Lissa," advised the Pilgrim. "She will hear Lydia's plea from millions of miles away and, just like me, she can travel swiftly through time and space. If you should call, you will suddenly have both of us there with you. But please remember: Do so only if you really need us!"

"That sounds very comforting!" I said, appreciatively embracing my friend. "Now I really do feel that it is time for us to seek out the unexplored regions of the Pleiades. Till we meet again, dear friend!"

I pulled Lydia up tightly next to me, and we both knew what we needed to think and say in order to shift environments. A moment is an age, compared with the time such a transition takes. So before we knew it, we were standing there, tightly embraced: two Angels on unknown ground, on a strange planet in the boundless Outer Space.

Lydia was the first one to pull away and wonderingly take a few steps, in order to investigate the surroundings. It didn't appear so very strange.

We were standing in a valley. There were high cliffs all around us, which made us feel more like we were in a deep pot. How were we to take ourselves out from there? But of course, we are Angels, so it went gallantly.

The sky above us was blue and there must have been a sun shining, for its happy rays reached down, searching us out through the cracks in the rock face and tickling our noses and mouths, which made us start to giggle.

"Ho ho, hello!" we heard a rather weak, high-pitched voice say from behind us. I turned around at the same time as Lydia. She gave out a little shriek and I flinched. A boy stood there, for it could not have been anything else. He was tall and thin, and had thick, bushy, dark hair. His eyes were unnaturally large, but I recollected having heard that the folk on the Pleiades were human-like, only with extraordinarily large eyes. He was clothed in tight, dark, short trousers that reached the knees, and a billowy white shirt. The boy exposed a white row of slightly pointed teeth and didn't look in the least threatening.

"Who are you?" he asked. "My name's Maris and my little sister's called Toya. Hey Toya, where are you? Come out this instant, do you hear? These are kind non-Pleiadeans; they aren't dangerous!"

A rustling noise came from behind a bush growing next to the cliff, and out stepped a smaller child, with equally large eyes and long, dark, frizzy hair. Lydia fell to her knees and took hold of the little sister's hands.

"Hello, Toya." She laughed. "We have just arrived here from Agartha. We just want to visit a little while and see what it's like on your planet. Do you live nearby?"

I don't rightly know why, but we Angels never seem to have any difficulty with languages. We were able to converse with no difficulty whatsoever, but don't ask me what language we spoke. Whatever it was we were speaking, I had to answer – and it always went very well. We'll leave that subject and speak as it comes.

"Yes, we'll take you to our mother," replied the boy. "Father is with the Ashtar Command all day long and we don't know when he'll be back, but mother is at home."

One corner of the cliffs jutted out a bit. I hadn't thought anything of it earlier, but concealed in the middle of it was an elevator. I quite simply hadn't noticed it, which was hardly surprising, since it was rather dark there. Maris lifted up his sister and rushed into the elevator. We hurried after him. He pressed a button, just as one does on Earth, and the elevator whizzed upwards. And it really did whizz! If I'd had enough time to think, I would have been panic-stricken and shaking like a leaf, but neither Lydia nor I managed to feel any reaction before the elevator shuddered to a halt.

Maris swished past us with his little sister sitting up on his shoulders. We shot off after him through the opened elevator doors, and the instant our feet passed through, the elevator zoomed back down. We followed on after our nippy little Pleiadean boy. Despite his burden, he moved incredibly swiftly. We noticed that his feet actually touched the ground, unlike the hovering movement in Agartha. Our feet stomped along in the normal way, also touching the ground – although Angels are of course lighter than ordinary human beings. I wondered if perhaps we had once again been embodied as humans. I gave Lydia a little random pinch as she ran past me (one must enjoy the moment of being human, however briefly!). She shrieked, which gave me the opportunity to physically give her a proper nip in the bum. Had she still been her Angelic-form she would not have felt it at all.

I eventually could see that we were running along a narrow woodland path, which in many ways likened to one in a Swedish wood. Possibly the trees were a little less dense here, and perhaps the fallen pine needles on the pathway were longer, thicker, and greener, but otherwise there appeared to be no great difference. Then we came out from the woods, but Maris didn't stop, and Toya continued playing at riding a horse on his shoulders. Some houses started coming into view.

On the Pleiades the houses weren't round, at least not in this star system. They weren't like ordinary houses on Earth either, apart from standing on the ground and having roofs. They were of various sizes and colors.

It's difficult, in a word, to describe houses that vary so much in size, color, and style. When Maris suddenly halted with a swishing noise, I immediately focused all my attention on that particular building. The sharply pointed roof incorporated the entire house. In fact, the roof reached all the way from the top, over the four walls, and down to the ground. It certainly looked rather odd, but I suppose one could become used to it.

"I have seen pictures of houses on Earth," said Maris, puffing and panting as he set his little sister down on the ground. "You have such peculiar roofs. Our roofs cuddle the houses, making them feel warm and cozy. Your houses let in both the cold and heat. We live in an embrace! Take a look around and you'll see what I mean."

I looked around and suddenly understood exactly what he meant. Lydia did likewise. The houses stood in short rows with streets running in between, streets lined with greenery. All the roofs were four-sided, reaching all the way down to the ground – but where were the doors and windows? There were no steps to be seen, either. When Maris saw the expressions on our faces, he fell about laughing; Toya, too! Most of the houses were square-shaped. A few larger ones were rectangular, and then I couldn't see any farther, since the alley came to an end. There was greenery to be seen everywhere: trees, bushes, and little shrubberies in front of some of the roofs.

To enter a house one, opened it up the same way one opens a garage door at home. The door lifted itself when Maris pressed a button, and he beckoned us to follow him in. In fact, it felt just like going into a garage, only it didn't smell of gasoline. It smelled lovely and fresh, of flowers – and something else that unmistakably had to be food. It was very light inside.

"You can come, too," said little Toya, and took Lydia by the hand. "Maris can look after the old geezer."

It seemed I was the "old geezer," I thought to myself, a little offended in my Angelic mind. But then I looked down and saw how my body appeared so completely solid and human-like. It had undergone change again. I sighed and looked around, sniffing at the pleasant aroma of food. My stomach grumbled, indicating I was definitely hungry.

I couldn't see any doors. The layout of the house towards my right seemed completely open. I could see some comfortable furniture that reminded me of that on Earth, also coffee tables and glass cabinets.

"Don't just stand there, staring!" Maris' little high-pitched voice squeaked. "Mummy wants you to come out to the kitchen. Lydia is already there eating!"

The last sentence immediately set my long legs into motion. I shot off after the boy and arrived in a deeply oblong, spacious kitchen. To the left was a large alcove with a table and chairs, where Lydia sat and grinned when she saw me. I almost ran into a woman, who politely halted me.

"You must be Jan!" she announced. "I'm the mother of these two little scoundrels. We say 'Mummy' or 'Mo' here. I can imagine that both you travelers must be very hungry. I was prepared for your arrival, so please, just eat up!"

The woman was tall and a little plump, with a most beautiful face and long, fair hair.

"Oh, by the way, my name's Gredine! You may live with us during your stay here. The Pilgrim sent us word of your pending arrival. The children were meant to collect you in the valley, but I can see how that only left you wondering; they are rather boisterous."

That's the least one could say, I was thinking, but just smiled, nodded, and promptly sat down next to Lydia. In a jiffy, a plate was set down on the table. Despite its thinness, the plate seemed to be made of stone, and the spoon was also of the same material. Served on the plate was a piping hot vegetable dish. Vegetarians here, too, I thought to myself.

On the Pleiades, one ate roughly the same sort of vegetables as at home, at least the taste was reminiscent of a mixture of Brussels sprouts, onions, and something else that was new to me. It was really delicious.

"When you have eaten your fill, you may take a look around our garden and rest for a while before my husband comes home," suggested Gredine. "I know he would like to speak to you and almost certainly will want to show you around here. We have small flying machines that work as well as your cars, but without putrefying the air."

The perfectly tended garden was astonishingly beautiful. It was full of fruit trees and bushes, and a vegetable garden containing a great variety of vegetables. Lydia flopped down onto a small bench and groaned, "Seeing all this makes me so terribly homesick. I loved planting seeds and watching them grow. Do you think we'll be taken around to see a little more of the town — if this is a town?"

"Patience, dear Angel!" I entreated, as I sank my teeth into a round, smooth fruit that neither tasted like an apple nor pear, but a sort of mixture of both. It was sweet, juicy, without spots, and very nice. "Well, they certainly do know how to grow fruit here," I muttered.

"Well, so do you on Earth, too!" retorted a chirpy voice, apparently coming from a tall, fairly sturdily built, blond-haired man, who suddenly appeared, coming down the garden path. "I am Peanon, Gredine's husband and good friend of the Pilgrim. Welcome, beloved guests!"

Peanon seemed an eminently convivial man, and before we knew it, we were seated in his very own craft of transport — he keenly emphasized "own craft," which was rather similar to the hovercraft in Agartha. I later was given to understand that these modes of transport varied greatly in design, just like cars on Earth.

"The Pleiades are comprised of many highly advanced, Galactic Societies that together form a brilliant star cluster," explained Peanon, while the craft calmly floated through the clear, balmy air. We saw the four-sided roofs, or should I say roof-clad houses, right up until the travel craft lowered itself down to land in an opening.

"We are now on a planet belonging to the Pleiadean star of Electra," he continued, "one of the stars you collectively call the Seven Sisters. We have no large cities like on Earth; we prefer smaller communities, where most people know one another and live happily together. Our culture is chiefly aimed at combining art with logic, which is probably an unlikely concept for Earth humans to be able to grasp."

74

"You can call us Earth-Angels," I interjected with a smile, and Lydia burst into a fit of laughter. Our host gave an appreciative nod of consent. He positively exuded an air of calm and dignity that I rarely had seen so elegantly combined with wisdom and humor. The Pleiades were really beginning to become a truly interesting star cluster.

12. A Pleiadean Parliament

Ahead of us lay a building that was larger than any of the others around us. But it, too, had a four-sided roof. Lydia called it a "roof-hug." Presumably this was an official building of some sort; its roof-hug was a myriad of varying, exquisite colors.

"This is our Parliament building," Peanon informed us. "If you like, we can refer to it as the Pleiadean Government House. In this place all decisions are made, laws passed, and orders given; it is here that all fields of consciousness that have not yet been utilized or are still lying dormant are activated. This is the very heart of the Pleiades. Step inside, my dear friends, please do come in!"

We stepped through the great, shimmering-colored "garage door" that glided up to expose an interior so brightly lit, we were forced to shield our eyes.

"You will become accustomed to the light," Peanon's soothing voice assured us. "You are now undergoing an edifying and beneficial radiation before stepping over the threshold. This is a necessary procedure for all visitors."

Lydia groped around to find my hand, and I tried to impart my confidence to her. I actually felt very safe, bathing in this powerful light, with all its loving warmth that sought its way through my entire body, irrespective of whether it was completely human or not. A moment in the cosmic light became a second of the life that was me right now. Peanon beckoned to us to follow him, and the instant we left the explosion of light, everything went back to almost normal again – if the fifth dimension can be counted as normal. I certainly didn't miss the third!

The floors and walls looked like they were made of marble in varying nuances of green and pink. I can't rightly say exactly what materials there are on another planet, which is why you will have to make do with me saying "looked like." Perhaps different materials aren't quite as different as one might think, when compared with those on Earth. Quite possibly all the planets have the same basis within geology as our Earth. So far it hasn't been possible to prove practically.

We entered a room, presumably an office of some sort. Every single wall was a computer screen, displaying various pictures. The occupants, all sitting at small, attractive tables, were pressing buttons on a strange machine that stood on every table, which I had never encountered before; they were neither like computers nor televisions.

"This is the room in which all communication with other planets takes place," our guide informed us. "The entire Universe is within our reach. But we must move on."

Since I didn't understand an iota of what I saw, and apparently neither did Lydia, we didn't hesitate to obey his summons. The pictures on the walls were in color, and some of them gave an eerie impression. They projected unknown species of beings, with virtually no resemblance to humans. But all those sitting in the room looked completely human.

The doors and windows looked like they were made of glass, just like at home, only the glass wasn't transparent. The ventilation was pleasant, so that one didn't feel shut in. We came to a corridor with beautifully patterned walls and doors made in the opaque glass. Peanon opened a door and we stepped through. Inside were a long table and seven comfortable chairs – which were in fact armchairs that were adjustable to suit the individual.

Peanon rang a little bell, which instantly summoned a gentleman and lady to the room. They also were humans, who were most attractive looking, if not exactly handsome. I would estimate they were middle-aged. Both were slim, of medium height, and had long, fair hair. They also both had dark blue eyes, but in all other respects were quite different from one another. The man was a little more powerfully built than the woman; he had bushy hair that stood straight up at the hairline, and a short beard. The woman had curly hair and was wearing a silky, bright yellow, shimmery tunic, while the man was dressed in blue. Apparently tunics and loose-fitting trousers were in fashion here, together with gold or silver sandals.

The lady was adorned with exquisite jewelry, so mesmerizing one could look only at it, forgetting all else. Around her neck was a thick, plaited gold chain with a pendant that glowed like a little sun hanging from it. From her ears sparkled diamonds, presumably, also round-shaped. Her arms were covered in various types of bracelets and she had rings on all her fingers. I furthermore noticed, despite Lydia's constant nudging, that she bore rings and bracelets on her feet and ankles, too. They were an odd couple, for even the gentleman wore jewelry, although not quite as lavish or massive as the lady's.

"Permit me to introduce my very dear friends, Solia and Solor, to the Earth-Angels, Lydia and Jan!" announced Peanon. Both gave a little bow, and we did the same in return. I saw how Lydia was desperately trying to repress giggling at the word "Earth-Angels," but was going to have to get used to it, because in this context, that's precisely what we were.

"You are now in one of the rooms where important decisions are made," continued our guide. "We have several such rooms. We work in clans, given different tasks to do. When they have been carried out, all twelve clans convene to make mutual decisions."

"It sounds simple, but unfortunately in practice it's rather complicated," Solor informed us. "The Pleiadean Star League is enormous, but on the other hand, there are never any complications once we have actually made our decisions. In the vast majority of cases we are unanimous."

"Men and women work together and respect one another," added Solia. "I know this isn't the case on Earth. However, the Earth is on the brink of a gigantic metamorphosis and it is our hope that women and men will subsequently become equals and respect each other's differences. We are aware that certain differences do exist between the sexes, and we always compensate for these on both sides."

"Women are the ones who give birth here, too, aren't they?" inquired Lydia.

The Pleiadean woman's responding smile was warm and loving. "Yes, of course, but we all help one another in every possible way. We know that sex is a somewhat popular pastime on Earth, but it is not at all so with us. We consider it a perfectly natural act between two individuals who love one another. We don't belabor the subject to the extent you do. We honor and respect it so that man and wife – as you say – enact sex for the purpose of producing offspring."

"So, do couples here remain married for life?" wondered Lydia.

Solia nodded. "Although we don't call it 'marriage,'" she couldn't help giving a little smirk, "we simply use the word 'partners' or 'betrothed,' or sometimes 'life companions.' No form of ceremony is necessary. If two people find they belong together then they know and act on it, and everyone else knows, too. 'For life' can be interpreted in many ways. We don't hop from one partner to another. If problems arise, then we find a remedy. There's a cure for all that is negative, for this is a Planet of Light."

"Phew!" gasped Lydia. "If only it could work like that on Earth."

"It will," assured Peanon. "There are many of us working on this. Great things are about to happen."

I, who am both old-fashioned and a freethinker, was feeling somewhat ambivalent, and I hastened to change the subject. "Do you hunt here?" I inquired. "Are there hunting grounds?"

Solor jumped up, leaving Solia's side. He stood right in front of me, staring hard into my eyes. "Hunting is what you do on Earth!" he angrily growled. "We eat neither meat nor fish. There are vegetables and fruit enough in our bounteous soil to feed the whole planet. You ought to consider this."

"I have actually never hunted and I am also vegetarian – that is, when I am in my physical state – otherwise, in my Angelic form, I don't eat at all," I retorted in a chilly tone.

"Sorry," mumbled Solor. "I took you for humans, but you are of course spirit beings who have come to study life here. I shall be happy to tell you. You have already seen how we live and perhaps understand that we exist very much like human beings on Earth."

"As it used to be on Earth," I corrected, "a long time ago. Now it is quite different there and extremely negative. That is the reason we are here: to learn more so that we can teach the humans on Earth how to live in a right and proper way."

"Do you have prisons?" asked Lydia. "Are any crimes committed here?"

"There aren't only seven stars, the so-called 'Seven Sisters,' as believed on Earth," replied Solor. "The Pleiades are numerous, but crime is unknown to us. Faults may occur, but whenever they happen, we set about rectifying them instantly. Thieves and murderers do not exist here. This sort of behavior practiced on Earth is an inconceivable concept to us, despite our being so similar in character."

"Punishment?" Lydia's characteristic doggedness caused all three Pleiadeans to momentarily fall about laughing.

"Regarding severe penalties (that are given extremely rarely) the culprit is sent to the outer edge of our planet and ordered to carry out various heavy, often dangerous jobs – for example, as a rock-blaster, cave-worker, or one who works below the surface of the sea," explained Solor. "But we naturally also have a number of boisterous youths who, of their own free will, enthusiastically seek out these jobs for sheer adventure. As long as this is done in a positive spirit, it is all to the good. It is the first thing an infant learns: to observe everything with happy, wide open eyes and to let the heart speak."

"Naturally, all our planets, whether great or small, work in a similar way. So if you've seen one, you've seen them all," added Peanon, resuming command. "Is there anything else you particularly wish to see?"

"Oh yes, please!" Lydia cut in before I managed to open my mouth. "I would love to see your schools!"

Peanon nodded approvingly and we took our farewells of Solor and Solia. Peanon's "own craft" of transport stood exactly where it had been left in the parking area, which was to be expected in a place where there were no thieves. We hadn't travelled very far, but came to an even bigger house, built right in the middle of a garden, or park, absolutely brimming with blossoming trees, bushes, and other plants. The roof "hugged" this building, too, and our guide opened the "garage-roof," just like before. A familiar sound reached our ears as we entered a hall similar to the one at the Parliament building. It was the unmistakable din of children's voices. Peanon opened a door and we stepped into the oddest schoolroom I had ever laid eyes on.

13. School System and Way of Living

The room was very large – in fact, extremely large. Everything was in great disarray, just as if the teacher was conspicuously absent. I reflected on such times as I remembered them, only this was far worse. When Lydia and I momentarily stood in the doorway in utter shock, trying to make out what was going on in all the noise, it suddenly fell silent. About ten children, who'd just been misbehaving like proper little rascals, sat at a round table, with two teachers facing one another. Order, calm, and concentration prevailed. Pleasant music, not in the least disturbing, channeled out from the roof, and the children looked like a group photograph – one of those taken to be kept safe and later shown to the grandchildren. All this occurred in an incredibly short time!

They were very nice-looking children, with big eyes and long brown or fair hair, shiny straight mantles of hair, and curly, frizzy wigs. Apart from the gentle music, there was absolute silence in the room.

"Hello!" said Lydia and I simultaneously. As if in response to a command, all the children stood up, bowed to us, and sat down again. Then they started to sing. The teachers hadn't taken the least bit of notice of us, but started conducting their little choir. It sounded quite heavenly (which of course I can tell, coming from a celestial abode).

The singing ceased and the children sat solemnly still while the two teachers, a man and a woman, stood up to greet us. I thanked them profusely for entertaining us so beautifully, and I asked about the method of teaching.

"We always have two teachers to every class," responded the male teacher. "The children study different subjects each day so that learning is constantly varied and fun. When you arrived we were just taking a little break, and then the children are encouraged to feel free. Please do look around!"

This we did, and apparently all the walls in the entire room were screens for film projection. They were used for both educational purposes and entertainment. When Lydia asked why there were only ten pupils, the female teacher replied that that was the maximum number permitted in a schoolroom. It was important that the children should become well acquainted and learn to get on with one another. The pupils were more attentive when there were only a few of them. Much of the education was conducted with the aid of the screens. There were dozens of little classes spread throughout the entire building, but there was only one big gymnasium, in which the children learned various movements of the body and their importance, besides dancing, music, and singing.

Lydia was absolutely delighted. "This is exactly how schools on Earth ought to be," she sighed.

However, I then wished to ask something quite different. "What do you do about religion?" I inquired as we were leaving the palatial school. "Do you believe in the same God as we do?"

Peanon gently smiled, nodding slowly. "I believe so," he replied. "After all, there is only one God, so you can't really choose any other, can you?"

"Churches, the priesthood? Popes? Bishops?" It was of course Lydia who was firing away these questions.

Peanon's smile broadened. "Let's take a little trip and take a look at how our religion works. The word religion isn't actually in our vocabulary; we just say 'faith.'"

He walked past our travel craft that was standing outside the school. "Come! A house for our faith is very close by," he said, as he went around the corner. We followed after.

A house just like any other house there, with the long four-sided roof down to the ground, came into view after a short walk. The difference was that this house was white. The roof was of shimmering gold. We hadn't seen any other white houses earlier, so this in itself was something new. The "garage door" (that I insist on calling it) swung up, enabling us to enter. We heard music as we went into an accommodating, but not oversized, room with low, comfortable chairs and sofas randomly placed here and there. A few locals sat, either alone or in company, while the music played a superbly beautiful melody. I didn't see an altar, but there was a podium at the farthest end, with a whole load of musical instruments. Among others, there was one largely resembling a grand piano. One could assume from this that performances took place here. We sat down on one of the sofas and Peanon sat opposite us.

Everything was white and gold. The walls glittered mildly and harmoniously. The floor was a mirror, just like the ceiling. The effect was strangely illusory. Peanon spoke in a very low voice. "This temple is a gathering place for those who wish to meditate awhile or ponder in peace and quiet – or simply relax," he explained. "You will find neither popes nor priests here, only harmony. There are no sermons, just music and beautiful singing. Sometimes performances are given – and little plays, too."

"If one has difficult problems, would one come here?" Lydia asked the question I had just been thinking.

"Yes, of course. There is always someone at hand here to help. Even children can come here. This place is instead of your psychiatric care. We do have hospitals, but they operate quite differently from the ones on Earth. Various methods of healing are a better alternative to pills, with all their side effects. Above all, they also work much quicker."

"If someone should die anyway?" A typical Lydia-question!

"No one lives forever in this physical reality, despite it being five-dimensional. What happens is that we are transferred to another dimension when we are finished with this one." Peanon smiled patiently. "You die in a different way, but I think our way is preferable. We know there is no final ending, just a transition, and humans on Earth ought to be able to understand this. Do you have any more questions?"

I managed to silence Lydia by giving her a cautionary glance, causing Peanon to continue smiling as he beckoned us to follow him. I suddenly thought of something: "Newspapers – do you have such things?" I hadn't seen a single poster put up anywhere, and no books or magazines lying on top of tables, either.

Peanon stood still in his tracks. "We have no need of newspapers, since news is constantly being updated and shown all day on the screens we have all over the place. However, we do have printing works to print books, because the people here prefer to read than see them in picture form, despite the screens being kept going all day. We like to make our reading sessions something of a special occasion, as we love to snuggle down into a comfortable sofa or armchair, munching some favorite sweets, when we open a book. We also have book houses where one may sit and read in peace and quiet, just like your libraries. This is where we can find books from Earth, too, translated into our own language. Of course, we can see films, but not like the ones you have, with so much violence and sex, etcetera. Our homes are extremely important to us, for it is in our homes that we truly develop."

"Do you play any sports?" I asked. "Do you compete in any particular fields, such as football or riding?"

"Competition is not a word that fits in here. It creates bad feelings." Peanon's voice sounded very grave. "We do have horses, and some camels and llamas that are suited to various types of territory and climate – which can be variable here, too. In some areas we use travel craft similar to the one I've been taking you around in. There are wilderness areas where wild animals roam and it is advisable to be protected."

"Do you go out on safaris?" I noted an underlying tone of irony in my Earth-Angel's voice, but this went unnoticed.

"We work to maintain good contact between people and animals here," was the curt reply, leaving no opening for further questions.

We left the chapel and hurried along to our trusty vehicle. "There are tunnels running underground in the Earth that one can travel through," I remarked, as we sat in the craft. "Are there such tunnels here, too?" I inquired.

"Yes, indeed, some can be found on a number of the Pleiadean star systems," replied Peanon. "They maximize the ease of transport on this planet, being so much quicker than your trains and cars. Velocities of up to 12000 miles per hour can be reached, converted into Earth speed.

We use other forms of measurement – I am sorry – but I have to say we apply mathematics and physics that are light years ahead of you!"

"I'm afraid you forget that we no longer are Earth beings," I gently pointed out. "But we must shortly move on to Sirius. Do you have anything more of interest to show us?"

"Well, yes – there are still a few things that could be useful for you to know. But this can be shown to you by film; otherwise it will take too long for us to travel all around, even if we increase the tempo. So let's travel back to the book house, where clear pictures and explanations are to be found."

14. Animal Life and Sea People

In no time at all, we were ensconced in the book house, in front of a white wall. Gradually it fluctuated between shades of green and blue before finally showing a picture.

First a house with a "hug-roof" and then the interior was revealed to us. The man of the house was sitting, doing carpentry next to a wide bench, while his son stood beside him, watching. The lady of the house was stirring something in a bowl, while her little daughter played with a little animal of some sort, possibly a squirrel, a bat, or a fox cub. The picture was entitled *An Evening at Home on Electra*.

Rather idyllic, I thought to myself, but somewhat old-fashioned.

The next picture was of either a stable or barn – or perhaps both, for it was large, long, and narrow. We looked inside the building and, just as I'd guessed, it was indeed a combined stable and barn. There were small horses – something like our ponies, but more strongly built. They had bushy tails and sturdy, furry legs. Peanon carefully turned one of them around, and I was startled to see the little horse's expression; it appeared so astoundingly intelligent, with big brown eyes and a mane that went all the way around its head.

"One has to trim their manes fairly frequently," Peanon informed us, "but don't they have the most adorable muzzles?"

Lydia was already there, stroking the muzzle of the animal, and then it pulled back and wrinkled its muzzle, giving the impression that it was smiling.

"He likes you," smirked Peanon. "But we must hurry on, because there are only small horses here. These small beasts are extremely strong, and we use them both in agricultural work and for pulling all sorts of carts. If, for example, one wishes to take a trip somewhere, one can call for one of these, which for us is the same as you calling a taxi."

"But you have your flying craft," retorted Lydia.

"Indeed, but sometimes we use horses, depending on where we live and what we are accustomed to," responded Peanon, giving the horse something that looked like a piece of bread.

We then continued. A long row of small horses in various colors presented itself. Some of them were actually a shimmering blue. We didn't see any larger horses.

We stepped over to another house in the row, which seemed extremely long; this one had dairy cows inside that weren't much like the ones we know. Oddly enough, on one side it very clearly smelled like a dairy, but the other side lacked any sign of milking activity.

"We see to it that the calves get all the milk they need, as far as we possibly can," explained Peanon. There were people all over the place, looking after the cattle. All of them smiled kindly at us and we smiled back. "Any excess milk is used purely in cooking and baking, in a form rather similar to your yogurt; which may be either natural or flavored."

"So do you bake like us – using flour, yeast, and spices?" Lydia once again put the question.

"Baking is universal," said Peanon, grinning. "However, refined grain won't be found here; we simply grind it, and that's all. Do we use yeast in baking? Why, indeed yes. All animals must have fodder, and animal-bread is fed to most species. We have goats and sheep, too, but they mostly graze freely in the mountain areas. But they keep an ear out to our signals, and hurry down to us if it sounds urgent. You must understand that all animals co-existing with and assisting us are extraordinarily wise and affectionate. Unlike you, we do not have dogs and cats as pets in the home, but wolves, otters, and suchlike instead."

Peanon must have seen my quizzical expression, and he giggled. "I lived on Earth at one period of my life," he explained, "which is why I am well-suited as a guide for, as in your case, ex-Earthlings. In case you're wondering if I was happy there, I can honestly say that almost no other planet in existence is as beautiful, although conversely the most evil. The inhabitants of the Earth must be awakened. The good and honest people must find a way to make the wicked see their folly so that they learn to be good, or be sent into exile. Rest assured that this is soon to be brought about!"

"I thought we were talking about pets," Lydia pointed out.

"Quite so; there is, in fact, a dog-like animal, ranging in size from very small to fairly large, and cats too, the latter being similar to the ones you are familiar with. But we do not have the vast variety of breeds, as on Earth. We do not experiment with the born traits of our cuddly pets, but accept them as Nature has intended them to be. It may surprise you to hear that we do eat fish, since they are in extreme abundance here and we have fishermen who love their profession."

"Oh goodness – I had almost completely forgotten to ask you about your seafaring!" I suddenly burst out. "Are there any boats here?"

The answer to this was an unadulterated, loud ring of laughter. Behind Peanon, the boy Maris suddenly popped up out of nowhere, and clapped his hands with delight. "Shall we take them out to sea before they take off to Sirius?" he cheekily asked our guide.

"But of course we have seas; this is a water planet, with practically too much water," replied Peanon. In a jiffy, we found ourselves out at sea with Peanon and Maris, while Lydia was swiftly transported home to Gredine, where a meal awaited her.

Sailing boats were apparently the most common here. I was taken off to the harbor, which one would hardly call small! It was chock-a-block with sailing boats – and others, too – none of which were motor-driven, but run on Zero Point Energy, which is the only form of energy used in the Pleiades, and many other planets. Our entire Universe is composed of Zero Point Energy, a fact which scientists on Earth have great difficulty in accepting.

In any case, it turned out to be a most wonderful boat trip, in what I considered to be a pretty normal sailing boat. The sea glittered rather more than one is used to on Earth, and the colors were as varied as those of a rainbow. Yet it didn't seem strange at all, but what did feel strange, however, was when an entity popped up out of the sea, swam towards us, and finally swung itself up over the guard rail, then spoke to Peanon and Maris in a completely strange language. The being had a human torso, but where the legs normally would have been, they looked as though they had grown together into a sort of fishtail. "It" – for I could not tell the gender of the being – had turquoise colored skin that was completely covered in scales, apart from its face, which was human-like, but with protruding eyes and a wide mouth, but whose nose was only rudimentary

"He belongs to the sea people," whispered Maris, who had obviously spotted my bewilderment.

I had read about mermaids, but never an entire race of sea people. I noticed he had gills, which looked most strange! This was without a doubt the strangest incident I had so far encountered, but evidently the sea people were of a friendly disposition. Peanon and the fish-like man chatted away enthusiastically until, finally, the fish-man came over to me, giving a kindly smile.

"Are you from Earth, where even the seas have been devastated by all the toxins?" he asked, in a language I was able to understand.

I shook my head and attempted to explain that I was from the higher spheres, which I'm not certain he understood. I furthermore did my best to let him know that his people did not exist on Earth, except in fairy-tales.

He obviously understood, since he laughed so heartily and yelled something out across the waves behind the boat. Instantly another member of the sea people popped up, only this time with a rather bounteous, scale-covered bosom. A sea-lady! She came straight up to me and stroked me rather wetly on the cheek. This was all a little beyond me; I hadn't the foggiest notion that there were any sea people in the Pleiades. Could there perhaps be trolls and other fairy-tale folk in the woods, too? I wondered.

"You do have myths about the sea people – or at least mermaids," announced Peanon when the peculiar pair of sea people dived back down into the waves. "It is almost certainly so, my dear Jan, that every myth has an origin in Truth. They cannot just pop up into one human's imagination, they must have a deeper background than people on Earth either suspect or even want to know. It's evident that people have built legends and altered other kinds of people to something other than they really are, attributed magic power to them and other abilities and traditions, including hateful qualities that don't even fit in. Anyway, enough on this, for I believe that at this very moment there is a most delightful meal awaiting us at my home, to be enjoyed before you and Lydia leave us and move on to Sirius."

We turned the boat about to head for home, and the wind was with us.

15. Sirius B at Last

(N.B.: Mariana Stjerna's visit to Sirius was a veritable experience. It occurred neither in a dream nor a vision. It was quite simply a memory she had had since early childhood, and she attempts here to recount the visit as precisely as she can. The memory has remained unchanged over the years and still feels very real to her. She frequently returns to the steps with the crystal gravel and has constant contact with Aranis.)

Once again I stood on unfamiliar ground, with a well-known head burying its nose in my shoulder and a recognized voice that whimpered, "Is it all right for me to look now? I can't keep my eyes so tightly shut much longer!"

"We've landed now, Lydia! You can open your eyes; we're standing up on a cliff." I had just managed to glance around and then let go of the narrow little waist that almost cupped exactly between my two hands.

My Angel friend rubbed her eyes and hopped around the edge of the cliff. "Is this Sirius?" She couldn't disguise the disappointment in her voice. "The same type of rock, same trees, same moss, although the colors are a little more varied and there are some small pink and white flowers. How pretty they are; like tiny stars!"

"Take a proper look, Lydia! This is only the landing spot, presumably for spaceships, although it's empty just now. Over there is a fence, and this here looks like it might be some sort of entrance from the plateau. Let's go over there and investigate!"

It was dark and shadowy farther beyond, behind the fence. The sun shone kindly onto the slightly damp ground and along the ledge of the cliff nearby. The ledge was interspersed deep into the cliff that rose high above us. I had discovered some steps that led a little way down to an elevator. It could only be an elevator, I deduced, since it quite simply looked exactly like an ordinary elevator on Earth. The doors stood open, and there was a strong light shining from within. I pulled Lydia into the elevator with me, but had no idea what to do next, since I could see no buttons to press. But before I even had time to think, the doors behind us closed and the elevator started on its descent, as steadily and smoothly as they usually do.

With a clonk, the elevator came to a halt. A concealed door glided open and we stepped out onto another plateau, much lower down and entirely different. We were out in a sunlit, astoundingly beautiful area. The first thing we saw was a road strewn with crystals, which coiled its way along and then disappeared around a turn to the left, a fair distance ahead.

The road glittered and gleamed to such an extent it made one's eyes smart, but one just had to become accustomed to the new, powerful, although strangely not unpleasant, light. Gingerly, we started along the crystal road. Both of us wore only thin, light sandals, yet it still felt oddly sacrilegious to tread on the sparkling crystal road. On the right side of the road it sloped downwards, not into a ditch, but the part of the cliff we'd been on and apparently walked along, which jutted out into peculiar, convex lenses that might have been windows. Down below gushed the bluest river I had ever seen, and across the other side of it a green-clad mountainside pointed its nose upwards like some giant animal, struggling to reach the air up in the blue heavens.

When we looked ahead, we saw someone hastening towards us. It turned out to be a rather tall young man. He smiled and waved to us with both arms. His fair hair was poker-straight, and cascaded down to his shoulders like a glossy curtain. His face gave the appearance of having been finely sculpted by a Greek sculptor; his physique was fittingly lithe and muscular. He was clothed all in white: trousers and a shirt, plus a short cape with gold emblems on the shoulders. The young man rushed up and warmly embraced us both.

"Welcome to Sirius, highly honored spirits!" he proclaimed. "We have received word of your arrival and mission here. One can have no secrets here!" he said and laughed. "You are on the road to the City of Hanging Terraces. Over here to the right you can see Mount Nymph, with its round windows. It is inside the premises behind those windows that scientists and inventors conduct their work. To your left is the Blue Horses' Meadow, as you can see."

Sure enough, to our great surprise, we instantly saw the glittering blue horses! There were both small and slightly larger ones, galloping around an enormous meadow. The left side of the road was a thicket of low-growing shrubs and lush bushes in bloom. Butterflies and bees, nigh on double the size of our ordinary Swedish ones, flitted and buzzed round about, sipping nectar from the large, exquisite, orchid-like plants. The vegetation was extraordinarily prolific, yet evidently limited by the meadow, which appeared to be a perfectly ordinary one in every way, apart from the interchanging color of the grass, just like the low-growing plants.

We drank in the wondrous beauty of the scene of this unusual landscape, but as the road took a sudden turn, we beheld a panorama view that was absolutely unbelievable.

"My name is Aranis, and I will accompany you throughout your stay here," announced the young man. "You now are able to more clearly see the City of Hanging Terraces before you. Below it runs the river, eventually ebbing out into the sea. The entire city is built in terraces."

It's not easy to accurately describe this suspended city. Behind it was a gigantic rock, like a wall that looked like some sort of great support for the terraces' extensive buildings, which appeared to plummet straight down into the river.

It was rather like a steep, wide, colossal stairway, wherein every step was composed of the most magnificent vegetation. Next to the stairway wall were dwellings that, despite their similar construction, differed greatly. Some had flat roofs, others sloping, while another variety were domed. One sort did not outshine another, but together combined to create a most wondrously beautiful impression. At the very bottom was a little marina (instead of a car park!) with boats of various shapes and colors. These were either sailing boats – some had multi-colored sails – or ones driven by energy unfamiliar to us, probably Zero Point Energy. The latter was evidently the most common form of energy of other planets.

Lydia and I walked on closely behind Aranis. It was a very long time since Lydia remained so silent! She was totally absorbed with all that she saw. There were people on the terraces. We didn't see them very close up, but as far as we could make out, they were handsome-looking and attractively built; they furthermore appeared rather happy. We heard singing and music, making Lydia unable to resist taking a few dancing steps.

Aranis gently smiled at her. "Do you like to dance?" he inquired. "For if so, you can dance to your heart's delight here on Sirius. This whole planet is a constant hubbub of singing, dancing, and music."

"What do you live on, then?" wondered Lydia in surprise.

"We precipitate everything we need," responded Aranis, still smiling. "That is to say, we create it with our thoughts. It is a form of mental power we learn from birth. Consequently, we require neither money nor banks – and not even shops. No one need feel envious of others, since everyone has all they require and the ability to create it."

"Superfluous question," I interjected. "Are you all vegetarians?"

"Naturally," retorted Aranis, somewhat surprised. "Aren't you? And we create our own food. However, this planet is shared by a large variety of ethnic groups; most have the ability to create, but a few have not yet learned the art and must attend school until they have perfected it."

"Are we going into the city?" asked Lydia. We were standing at the glimmering, shiny, high city gates, made out of something that looked rather like silver, with stones like bricks out of glass.

"No, not glass!" chuckled Aranis, obviously a lad with a happy disposition who was able to read our thoughts. "They're made of clear quartz – otherwise called rock crystal. They glitter so beautifully in the sunlight. But let's continue on to the Inland Temple; we'll take a look at the city and the Rock Temple later. There's no performance until this evening, and then we must go through the city to get to the boat going to the temple. Come along now!"

Reluctantly we left the sparkling city gate and followed our newly found friend along the sun-glittering gravel. So far we hadn't seen any vehicles, but on the other hand, it felt natural and effortless to walk around the place; each step trodden seemed soft and light, taking us a good bit forwards.

"I feel like a kangaroo!" Lydia piped up, reaching out for my hand. Instantly Aranis grabbed hold of her hand so that she floated between us like an enchanted reed. We at least managed to take a look at the plants bordering the crystal road.

We watched the blue horses in their meadow for quite a long time. They giddily galloped round and round, snorting and neighing so that the moisture from their breath spouted out like sprays of glittering pearls. These were happy horses that had a good life, I thought to myself. Suddenly we reached the end of the Blue Horses' Meadow. On the left side was a wood, sparse and ethereal as a midsummer night's dream. Directly in front of us was a high hill with narrow steps cut into the ground, which were overgrown with moss and short grass. Upon lifting one's gaze, a temple could be seen up at the very top, which was round, shimmering gold and white, and encircled by ornately carved pillars. It was so exceedingly, breathtakingly beautiful!

16. A Conversation with a Wise Man

We entered, all three of us holding one another's hands. Aranis was in the middle; he was our support. Without him everything was just a great, daunting, unfamiliar labyrinth. His light, lithe manifestation, with happy, playful, clear blue eyes, couldn't possibly frighten anyone.

We went into a circular hall with the most exquisitely ornate walls. In the center was a spiral staircase, which led to the floor above; where the open bannister revealed nine doors. It occurred to me that I had seen something similar earlier on our travels. Perhaps the holy temples were similarly formed on several planets. Most people – as far as I could understand – prayed to the same God: the One, First Source of all Creation. In which case, by definition, the same atmosphere, the same air breathed into the same type of lungs, the same feelings impressed into the same hearts and, of course, the same Love, must be spread from one and all beings. At least that's what I thought.

Aranis looked me deep in the eyes. "You do understand!" he declared. "Here exist only those who understand, and when we all are gathered together, the understanding accumulates to a staccato that can be heard across the entire Universe. Come with me!"

The spiral staircase took us up to the floor above. When we alighted it, we ascended in less than a second. Aranis opened one of the nine doors and indicated to us to step into the room. I almost jumped back in shock, for the room was jam-packed with books, files, and scrolls that looked as though they would surely topple over on us.

Amidst all the heaps of books was a wide, golden-yellow table, at which a small man could be seen sitting at the one end, deeply engrossed in something that looked like a map. Aranis strode up to him and tapped him gently on the shoulder.

"Master Ponteos, arise from the amber table! We have guests from the higher dimensions, Jan and Lydia, bearing greetings from The One!"

The little man shot up as though fired from a gun and stared at us somewhat confusedly. Despite his small build, there was an air of grandeur about his person. His head was almost bald, apart from a few long white strands straggling around it. His beard was also rather sparse and dirty white, hanging down to his corpulent stomach. His eyes were amber-colored, like the table, and he had a small mouth with narrow lips that turned upwards at the corners, as though constantly smiling. He looked at us from one to the other, then took hold of both my hands and flashed a broad grin, revealing an even row of white teeth.

"Welcome, dear honored guests; welcome indeed!" he burst out in his guttural voice, and at the same time shaking my hands so hard that I feared they would break off at the wrists. He then turned towards Lydia and bowed so deeply that his skull brushed the floor.

"Charming lady, welcome into my humble place!" he announced softly. Then he folded his arms across his chest and alternated scrutinizing glances from one to the other of us. "And to what do I owe the great honor of such esteemed visitors?" he boomed in quite a different voice, which sounded perfectly clear and concise.

Aranis spoke before I managed to answer his question. "These two Angels have been sent from Heaven in order to see how we live here on Sirius, Your Grace!" he declared, bowing courteously. It was just like watching a scene from an eighteenth-century play. The little old man was dressed in knickerbockers of variegated gold brocade, a ruffled yellow shirt, and a waistcoat that shimmered like gold, but – to be perfectly honest – looked as though it had seen better days. His narrow, black silk shoes with slightly upturned toes were rather shoddy and coming apart in several places. Who was this old fuddy-duddy? I wondered.

"I am 'The Omniscient' Ponteos; that is to say, I am an all-thinking, all-knowing, and all-pragmatic wise man, if you like. I am furthermore a veteran soothsayer and I have predicted, via my solar friend here, that two from the very highest would be dispatched to me very soon. It has to mean you; look at this!" He swiftly dug out a large crystal ball from under a layer of documents. This had to be his solar friend, I mused.

Lydia still held her silence, but smirked while remaining concentrated on all the old man's actions. He placed his hands on the crystal ball, after having first blown a thick layer of dust off it.

"I have here all the books there are on Earth and many other planets, too," he informed us, "besides which," he continued, "those I don't have here, I can procure via my solar friend, who tells me all I wish to know – and often a little bit more."

We watched while the entire surface of the large ball rippled, darkened, and was penetrated by flashing rays and finally displayed the celestial sphere – or a constellation in which Sirius shone the brightest.

The old chap gave a snort and then grunted, "The Earth cannot even be seen. Dear oh dear, is it possible that the metamorphosis has already commenced? I suppose you are aware that your beloved Earth is heading for an overwhelming change from without to within – or should I perhaps say it the other way around?" he tut-tutted.

"We came to you, Master Ponteos, in hope of gaining a little more information about the Earth," interrupted Aranis. "We already are well aware that the Earth is the current focal point of the entire Galactic Federation. We know that something overwhelming is to occur there. It is also clear that Mother Earth's affliction is unbearable and will have to be cured. We furthermore know that Heaven is taking an active part in the necessary changes being carried out. We do not wish to hear more about the deeds of the dark Cabal; people on Earth have already been hard hit enough by them. But we would very much like to learn about the entry of the Light, the revival and consequent rejuvenation that is to take place. The space above Earth is full of armies from the planets of Light and Love that are busy arming themselves in preparation for the troubled times ahead, by gathering valuable information in order to assist and advise humankind. What draws nigh is the great cosmic battle to banish all evil from the regions pertaining to Earth and its people. The Ashtar Command, Alpha Ship, and many more are waiting ready to defend and save all the righteous and just people. The change will be immense, immeasurable, and – by the human race – unexpected, but absolutely necessary if we are to reveal our existence and participation to the Earth. We shall be met with much fear."

"On every planet, including the Inner Earth, we have come across the very same vision of the future," I humbly declared. "What do you think you are able to do from here to help the people of Earth?"

"A very great deal!" proclaimed the elderly man. "You cannot imagine the great amount of preparation we have going on from all the constellations in the Sirius complex. You will soon be shown how things work for us on Sirius and thereby better understand how your Earth can positively develop by putting into practice the right philosophy of Love and Justice. This Universe is enormous, if not the hugest. But we can, we are able, and we will! It was perhaps to hear just these words that you came to me."

"How do we get people to purify their thoughts?" asked Lydia. "So many attempts have been made, and we no longer even exist on Earth. We cannot influence anyone to guard their thoughts. The children are disturbed so much by all the misery that they are unable to think of anything other than themselves, taking to hatred and revenge whenever they feel necessary. This is the accepted way in many countries. They believe that God is a harsh judge who punishes and disapproves. Can we ever change this?"

"We certainly can," Ponteos said most decidedly. "New teachers are to be trained, which is already in progress. The changes will be so disruptive that all doubt will be dispelled. Your mission here was to ascertain whether Sirius has both the authority and ability to perform miracles of Love. Run along now with my young friend, Aranis, and you shall see in greater detail how it works for us here. I can sit here indefinitely, telling you all about what is going to happen, but it's not a very good idea. Farewell, dear messengers from on high, and please take back with you to Heaven all my blessings and Love."

The funny old man made a curt bow to Lydia, then did the same to me. Immediately thereafter, he returned to his studies in the dusty corner and appeared to once again be fully engrossed in reading his documents. Aranis beckoned us to follow him. The audience was concluded.

17. Heading to the Dolphins

"We have just met the wisest man of this Universe," declared Aranis, when we had reached the bottom of the spiral staircase once again.

"It was rather a brief visit," retorted Lydia. "We were told nothing new, either."

"But *is* there anything new regarding this most important question?" returned Aranis wonderingly. "Perhaps you may think so after we've been around all the places I will be showing you."

I cast a questioning glance at the remaining eight doors, causing Aranis to burst out into laughter.

"No, Jan, we are not seeing any more wise men here just now. We are going to pay a visit to the dolphins. They have their headquarters over the other side of the Great Mountain. We'll take the shortest route, by sea, which will require travelling in a special vehicle."

We had gone out through the magnificent city gate when Aranis blew into a small, glittery gold whistle. I was just thinking it was a bit old-fashioned to use a whistle, but the thought had hardly entered my head before a ship stood in front of us – and what a vessel it was, too! It likened to neither car nor a boat. In fact, what it did look rather like was a little spaceship, an upside-down saucer with a flat undercarriage, upon which there was a propeller and other dangling gadgets that I could make neither head nor tail of.

"For landing with, of course," commented Lydia coolly, and clambered up a ladder that folded down from the edge. I followed her lead. Aranis was already at the top, and the ladder was immediately propelled back up. A door swiftly shut behind us as we entered into something a bit like a comfortable, pleasantly decorated aircraft cabin. Without so much as a glance in my direction, Lydia went and sat by a window at the very front. I sat at a window on the opposite side. After an incredibly speedy and silent journey, the sound of water splashing up against the side of the vessel suddenly became audible. Aranis presented us all with some strange kind of headgear looking like a sort of helmet with gills.

"We shall be spending some time under sea and inside a vacuum room, which is why you need to be properly equipped to enable you to breathe for an unlimited time."

"Will we be spending a long time with the little fishy-wishys?" chuckled Lydia, which made me really cross.

"Now you just behave yourself!" I barked. "Dolphins are not fish – they're more humanlike than humans themselves! I am ecstatically overjoyed at being given this opportunity to go to them; it's the most exciting part of this entire expedition."

Aranis, who up until that point had been standing silently, listening to our dispute, smiled and interjected, "They are a people – just as we are a people – and both happily co-exist on Sirius. We consider the dolphins to be our brethren. Their dominion is rather damp, which is why we need the helmets, so you'll be able to hear what they say while protecting your ears. Better folk than these are scarce to find, Lydia. Admittedly they are a little different, but on the other hand, you have a multitude of different races on Earth and other planets, and much of your expedition is about learning how they may harmoniously co-exist. It isn't skin-color, physical appearance, or language that defines human behavior, it is the inner self that is crucial."

"Sorry," was all Lydia said.

We didn't feel a thing during our air trip, so it surprised me when I heard a little thud and Aranis, who'd been sitting right at the front at some sort of instrument panel, stood up and announced that we had arrived. The inwardly inclined door opened up and we put our helmets on. We climbed out onto a rather slippery algae track, straight into the green glow of a sort of swimming light. We were on a seabed, or perhaps a coral reef, since there were small mounds of coral all around us. Aranis blew a short signal with his whistle and our vessel vanished. Our guide was also wearing a similar sort of diving helmet to ours. When I touched his arm, it didn't feel the least bit wet. Lydia grabbed hold of my arm and I heard her astonished gasp that I was dry. Apparently there really were ears built into the helmet!

Aranis, as usual, led the way; this time we floated in amongst the aquatic plants, surrounded by a turquoise light.

"The light is the same, both where the dolphins and the sea people are," said Aranis. Speaking through the helmets seemed to work well, although I have no idea how. We just spoke as normal and could hear one another's voices perfectly well. The sea people, I wondered – what did he mean by that?

"He of course means the amphibians. You know, the ones ruled by Oannes, and about whom the Dogons – a West African people in southeastern Mali – had carved their encounters into the cliff walls after the amphibians from Sirius had visited them," jabbered Lydia, without stopping to draw breath, making her cough. Aranis bade her be quiet and then pressed a button that supplied her with more air to breath.

"You won't have to have these, once we reach our destination," Aranis consoled us. "You are not used to these helmets, and Lydia probably didn't press the right button to replenish the oxygen. I did indicate where it was when you put them on, but I can understand how exciting this all must seem to you, being very much outside the ordinary power of Angels." He rounded off this sentence with a soft little peal of laughter and then continued, "I thought you knew all about the amphibians, especially since Mariana Stjerna has given a perfectly lucid and substantiated account of them."

"Not to me!" contradicted the mouth inside Lydia's helmet. "May we hear it before we get there?"

"Okay, I'll ask her," I said, and that was how we came to be standing in a load of kelp and other seaweed, while taking a break so that Mariana could tell us about it.

18. Mariana's Nocturnal Amphibian Visitation

I am now exceedingly old, but the incident I am about to recount, that I experienced as veritably substantial, occurred in my late teens, when I was about eighteen or nineteen years of age, i.e., in the 1940s.

I was asleep in my bedroom, in my parents' house in Björkhagen, Stocksund, Sweden. My bed stood with the foot half of it protruding slightly out of an alcove. I was rather vain in those days (verified by Janne) and had rolled my hair up on curlers.

I suddenly awoke and sat up in the bed. A strange light shone in from the door that opened up onto the landing. Someone, who conveyed the light, had stepped in through the door and gone straight to the foot of my bed. I stared hard, and clearly saw an extremely tall man standing there, with legs akimbo – one on either side of the bed. Goodness, how big and tall he was! He was all scaly, right up to his neck. Above the iridescent green coloring of the fish scales was a human face. He had a broad, straight nose, large dark eyes, and an ordinary human mouth. I can still see him in front of me, for I had never before in my life ever felt such overwhelming Love emanating from anyone. Half dazed, I took the curlers out of my hair and laid them on my bedside table, in evidence that he had been there. He gently smiled, walked straight across the foot of the bed up to the window, and disappeared through it.

The following morning, the curlers lay exactly where I had put them on my bedside table, and the memory of the amphibian man (that I didn't then know he was) has never left me. Beneath our house Edsviken bay flowed down to the estuary, and in my mind's eye I saw him disappear there. Only how? That still remains to be investigated. The curlers gave me undeniable proof that I had been awake and lucid at the time of my visitation. But why did this happen to me? Perhaps it was because I was meant to tell you about it now?

This is not the only "supernatural" incident that has happened to me, but no one believes me, even though I tell the Truth. Many people doubtless think, "Gosh, how dreadful it would be if supernatural things really did happen!" It was precisely the same then as now: Far too few can accept that the Earth encompasses both what we can and cannot see with our physical eyes. The day will come when proof of this will be made so apparent and obvious that humans will feel embarrassed that they never dared believe it.

19. The Dolphin Community

We shall now resume Jan and Lydia's visit to the amphibians and dolphins.

"Let's go to the dolphins first! We're already there!" Aranis called out. "Once we're inside, you can take your helmets off. Just follow me!"

Clearly a form of door or entrance existed, since Aranis swiftly slipped through, closely followed by Lydia and me. We found ourselves inside an expansive, bluish chamber.

We removed our helmets and placed them on a stool that Aranis pointed at. We breathed freshly and easily. There was fervent activity round about us. A great number of dolphins swam around us in a strange sort of atmosphere that was neither air nor water, but most definitely a special "dolphinosphere." We could breathe exceedingly well there. Aranis was busy paying his respects left and right; some dolphins he kissed on the nose, others he just patted. A hubbub, which must have been the dolphins' chatter with one another, buzzed around us.

There apparently was another chamber within the chamber. We walk-swam-floated into it.

As you certainly are aware, dolphins are large beings. We felt very small in these chambers, but were surrounded by an extreme kindness that penetrated deep into our hearts. We passed a room that evidently was some sort of play-school for the little dolphins. It was great fun to see how these happy little bundles obediently followed the guidance of a mastodon character, which apparently was their teacher. There were a number of instruments in the room that were impossible for me to make out – and perhaps I wasn't meant to. Aranis urged us to continue onwards. In the next room there were unmistakable dolphin police – or whatever one might call them.

Aranis explained, "The dolphins who are sent down to Earth

can meet with a terrible fate. I expect you know this. They therefore train special types of police and guardians who are to help people in various ways, but also guard one another. There are so many pitfalls. Some dolphins deliberately expose themselves to evil to act as a kind of martyr. A number of humans are excessively wicked and brutally cruel, particularly in the northern part of the hemisphere, willfully forcing the dolphins, who are in every respect good beings, to endure great suffering. In such cases, the dolphin police have no chance at all. Many of them freely put up with torture and death in order to be able to accompany their comrades back home to Sirius B. Once at home again, both the sick and the dying are administered the most fantastic healing process. This is an area in which the dolphins excel."

The dolphins here lead a rich family life. They belong with one another for as long as they live. We saw several such well-bonded families. The matriarchs appeared very loving and protective of their dolphin young, as they played their unruly diving games close by, keeping a watchful eye on them. The family members spoke to one another by sounding a variety of tones, which one can assume is their proper dolphin language.

Aranis led us further along through the blue shimmering caves, till we arrived at a hospital. There were no beds to be seen, of course, but the sick and wounded dolphins were lying down on soft mats of seaweed and were, quite evidently, being treated both skillfully and effectively by other, healthy dolphins. Aranis explained that all adult dolphins were highly efficient healers; they were taught the techniques from early childhood.

"Who rules the dolphins?" demanded "Miss Curiosity" Lydia.

"We're just on our way," was the reply Aranis gave. So we walked (swam, floated) into a chamber that was very different from the others.

"The dolphins are so meticulously well organized that it is easy to see that they can neither belong to the Human nor Animal Kingdom. Let us instead call them 'Higher evolved beings.'" Aranis' voice sounded deeply reverent and I, too, felt the same as I beheld the grandeur of this new chamber, the splendor and perfect order of it. Everything was arranged in circles. Within the innermost circle sat (or lay) two extremely large and powerful dolphins, the one slightly smaller than the other.

"Our Royal Couple!" announced our guide by way of an introduction, whereupon instantly seeing us, the regal two jumped up to greet us. They waved with their fins and laughed heartily. Dolphins really can laugh and are the living proof of the vast, all-encompassing Love that prevails over their kingdom. They called out something guttural to Aranis as the Royal Couple's closest members dispersed to make a pathway between them. Aranis beckoned to us to accompany him in going to them. The regents were excessively adorned, with jewels hanging around both head and neck. This looked a bit silly, I imprudently thought to myself.

Aranis, as usual, read my thoughts, but simply smiled a little apologetically. "There has to be some recognizable way of singling out the rulers of the people," he whispered to me. "This is the chosen way, at least for special occasions when they stand in ceremony – and today is one such day. This special feast day is held in honor of your coming to visit them from the higher realms. Everything here is carried out most democratically. So please just wave and bow, if you would be so kind!" This we did.

The Royal Couple were surrounded by at least fifty dolphins. Aranis explained that these were counselors; they jointly solved all problems without ever being at loggerheads.

The Queen rose and went forward to Lydia, bowed down, and caressed her with her nose. In a flash, Lydia responded by stretching herself up on her toes and returning the caress with little kisses and pats, as best she could, while trying to reach up to the great head. Lydia never held back her demonstrations of Love. I was a little more reserved – or as Lydia would have put it, snobbish. It is with great regret that we were not able to converse with these marvelous beings, and I vowed I would study the dolphin language the moment I returned home to our dimension. Aranis, however, conversed with them fluently. The audience was soon over and we went back through all the chambers and recovered our helmets.

"You can tell Heaven that the dolphins are its most humble servants," conveyed Aranis. "There prevails perfect order, light, and an atmosphere of Love over everything, unerringly. They are not angry with you for the current atrocious executions of dolphins, despite all prohibitions and warnings. They understand, forgive, and heal. Soon it will all come to change, they say. The evil humans we call the Cabal will be exiled to another planet while the Earth is undergoing its 'purification.' Penance will be imposed and schools arranged for the Cabal, in which they will be unable to avoid betterment and contrition. This entire Universe will be God's good creation in a good world. It is to this end that we are working, in an organization in which most planets participate with their Space fleets.

"However, we shall now pay the sea people a visit, where Oannes rules. It was he whom Mariana saw in her teenage vision, although she may not have realized this. So now she will in mind join the three of us, and learn exactly who the amphibians are."

20. Visiting the Amphibians

"According to an old legend, it was Oannes who was the founder of all civilization on Earth," said Aranis, as we stepped into the vessel awaiting us outside the dolphin city. "However, the atmosphere around his people was very like that of the dolphins, so that his kingdom – as far as the air and civilization were concerned – was reminiscent of the dolphin one, but also similar to the human one. Despite there being many amphibians inhabiting the Earth these days, human beings do not believe in them. You will now receive proof that they exist just as much as the Earth's ordinary, accepted inhabitants."

The minute we stepped out of the vessel, we realized we still were at the bottom of the sea. Aranis bade us put on our helmets. Just as before, we then proceeded to traipse across the sand. This time it may have been a little less overgrown, with fewer aquatic plants, but we were surrounded in the exact same turquoise light. We walked straight through an enormous cave, where little fishes swam around in light that streamed in from somewhere. There was a door inside the cave. Aranis knocked on it three times, whereupon a man opened it. For the benefit of the reader, when I speak of men and women, I wish to describe their appearance, in order to help you understand and picture them. Everyone streamed towards us from the opened door, nodding and smiling.

They basically all looked very like ordinary people, but somehow more old-fashioned than we are used to. Their skin was smooth and very pale, their eyes weren't at all dark, but in various, light – mostly green – nuances, and their mouths were quite large, with fairly thin lips. Their arms and legs were very like ours, apart from them mostly being tucked into a fish-suit that all seemed to be part of the scale-covered skin. I never succeeded in ascertaining whether the scales on the skin were an integral part of the whole body, or drawn over in the way we pull on stockings. That they were built like humans was obvious. One didn't see a great deal of their hair, since the fish-hood of the suit was invariably pulled over the head. The men's faces were bearded. Furthermore, there were other beings, looking exactly like fish, that could walk upright on powerfully-built fishtails. Truly singular folk!

The dolphins and the amphibians constituted a remarkable unity, as they moved around in the chamber we entered. I made it my priority to closely observe the inhabitants there. I was beginning to tire of all the beautifully adorned caves that we'd seen so many of. The planets both Lydia and I had visited were full of caves. I think there must be a lot of mountains on most planets, and consequently inhabitants everywhere have sought out the natural caverns therein.

Aranis tugged at my sleeve. "Here are our rulers," he said.

Just as in the dolphins' Royal Chamber, the amphibians' Royal Couple sat at the end of a long table, seemingly prepared for a banquet. It was laid with plates and goblets, set before each person, and the table was piled high with various dishes of fruit and other food.

The Royal Couple were not like the dolphins. They were magnificently dressed in fish-suits, but their heads and bodies were entirely human. The only thing that wasn't human about them was that they had gills where the ears normally would have been. However, the Queen had a mass of greenish curls that acted to conceal these, and both she and the King bore crowns of pearls that were delicate and exquisite masterpieces of goldsmith handicraft. They wore long cloaks that glowed with a subtle light emitted from every crease, which created a rather beautiful, though peculiarly unreal, atmosphere. This thought sprang to my mind even though I, strictly speaking, was myself unreal, but in that moment I seemed to have forgotten it. In fact, the whole situation was an entirely new concept of reality to us, and I could see how Lydia, too, was totally mesmerized by the sight of it all. I can't exactly say what material the wide thrones with high backs were made of, but it looked like exceptionally intricately crafted gold filigree.

The Royal Couple arose and embraced us both. It was almost like a perfectly ordinary, human hug, only perhaps a little more airy. Faint music filtered down from the high ceiling, as light, soft, acoustic waves.

"You, who represent the Human Kingdom of Earth, are indeed most welcome," announced the Queen, smiling gently. "You will, of course, dine with us?" she gestured with her hand, and instantly two extra places appeared laid at the table, one for me next to the King and one for Lydia, at the Queen's side. We gingerly sat ourselves down upon the delicate, ornate chairs, having momentarily forgotten that we, too, were currently of a flimsier constitution!

"You doubtless wish to know a little about how this part of Sirius is governed?" proclaimed the King quizzically, while giving me a friendly thump on the back. "It's not very complicated, you'll see. The Queen and I each have our own council; both are composed of twelve members. We confer with them on all issues, and subsequently all meet for a final discussion. Disputes naturally do occasionally arise, but are immediately settled by vote or debate. We are most interested in hearing the opinions of the people, so elected public representative votes are always taken into account. In this way we always avoid political disorder. Should a situation of reluctance, envy, or evil arise among the leading ranks, this would be swiftly quashed; not, however, by using any form of violence. It is our policy here always to apply reasoning in such matters, and most often either the Queen or I personally take on the task of speaking to the unhappy individual concerned. The act of speaking reason is a most effective method of solving problematic issues, and is widely adopted everywhere – except on Earth."

"Do you have any sort of banking system?" I queried.

The King burst out laughing in response. "Yes, one can certainly say that we do," he smilingly proclaimed. "The best banking system one can imagine is not to have any banks at all, and to dispense with the use of money. That is how it is here, and so also on most other planets in Outer Space. We have the ability to create most things by thought, since the Divine Law of Abundance listens and grants us what we wish for. It surprises us immensely that the Earth exists in a system based on money. Money begets envy, competition, greed, and never-ending comparisons, being a perpetual source of discontent. You will find none of this here. When will the human beings on Earth have the insight to come to understand this?"

"I have heard that things are happening on Earth," said the Queen with a knowing smile, putting her arm on Lydia's shoulder. "Great changes are required there, and great changes will come to pass, seeming as though all hell is breaking loose. So what do you think of that?"

"We are aware of this, and almost certainly this is the main reason why we have been sent on this mission," responded Lydia swiftly. "We are here to learn as much as we can, in order to pass on our knowledge to the Earth. But since we no longer are human beings, our positive experiences will have to be channeled through our good contacts there. There must come a time when they will have to start to listen and try to understand what has to be done. I think that time is coming very, very soon."

We were silenced by the fabulously delicious food, made from all the choicest vegetarian delicacies of the sea. Everywhere we went where we were able to eat, we were served an abundance of wonderful varieties of vegetarian dishes. The karma of animals here did not include being devoured by humans. To them we clearly were cannibals. They lived and died naturally, and Nature itself is sufficiently wise to sow its own seeds. I gave a deep sigh. I didn't need to ponder the lack of understanding of humans. It was a long time since I had been a human. I suddenly thought of a rare, bloody steak, and felt quite sick. If only people were capable of personally experiencing the miserable suffering that animals go through prior to their slaughter, perhaps they would cease to eat meat.

After supper, we accompanied the Royal Couple on a tour around the annexing caves, in which they grew their crops. It was quite magnificent. We even saw how the amphibian children lived. I firmly believe many human children would be filled with envy if they could see them, for these were surely the happiest, really rather bubbly children I had ever seen all at once. Whenever their liveliness became a little too noisy, a signal was heard, whereupon the mischievous ones immediately fell silent. There were games and toys I had never seen before. There were swings and trampoline-like jumping devices, and always assisting adults present to lend a helping hand. The children sang and played odd, small instruments, similar to flutes and violins, only with buttons and strings. The music sounded gentle and lovely. They also danced, either by themselves or together. Indeed it was, without a doubt, quite the most harmonious school I had ever seen.

"There is someone waiting for you here," said the Queen, taking Lydia under her arm. We headed back to the throne room. Before even managing to enter, a wild barking sounded from within, and something shot straight at Lydia, causing her to topple over. She was unable to stand up again, because a coarse tongue was licking her all over her head.

"Lissa!" she shrieked, hugging the dog almost to death.

"Pilgrim!" I yelled, thumping him all over the place, in extreme joy at seeing him again.

He pulled both Lydia and me towards him. "Come, we must hasten to the surface; you cannot remain here any longer!"

Behind him stood Aranis, who yanked Lydia free from the dog's excited somersaults. We took our farewells from the lovely monarch couple somewhat curtly, and within a minute we were once again standing with our feet on terra firma, removing our helmets.

21. The Stairway Restaurant

"Are you hungry?" inquired Aranis before we managed to climb up into the vessel behind him. Indeed, I was perpetually hungry when in physical form, and therefore just about to say "Yes," when Lydia first yelled a resounding "No!"

Our stomachs were apparently not in tune with one another, but I chose to remain silent. Aranis and the Pilgrim sat opposite us; Lydia's lap was filled with a large dog.

"You are to participate in something unique," said the Pilgrim, "which is the reason why I came here. Partly I wanted to talk to you a bit about your continued journey, and partly I wished to be present for the Evensong in the Ivory Cave. The latter takes place only once per year, and last time I missed it."

"Why so seldom?" demanded Miss Inquisitive. "Why don't you have Evensong more frequently? Just like on both Earth and in the Heavenly Spheres. Are they not songs in praise of the evening and the Divine?"

Aranis smiled meekly and answered, "Our Evensong may not correlate exactly with yours. Of course it is a song of praise, but with greater depth and more powerful character. It is a method of purification in preparation for the night's dreams, a sort of Nature's own performance." With a little gasp, Lydia burrowed her head into the dog's bushy mane of fur, and I knew she was trying to suppress an attack of the giggles.

In an attempt to cover up for her, I hastily said, "We are so very much looking forward to experiencing this rare occasion, and having the opportunity of learning something new that can be of great value to our friends when we return home."

"We shall be disembarking very shortly," announced Aranis, just as the vessel's undercarriage touched the ground with a loud bang. Despite this noise, the landing felt completely soft and smooth. We stepped out onto a terrace set with tables and chairs. Both Lydia and I hurried over to the beautifully floral-adorned fence on the one side and leaned over it. Down below us was another terrace, and below that I glimpsed another, and I understood that it was the terraces of the City of Hanging Terraces, which we had seen when we arrived on Sirius.

"Kindly sit down!" commanded Aranis. "We are early, so I thought we might eat something before making our way into the mountain."

I glanced downwards and caught sight of the bluest of blue water, with loads of funny little boats bobbing up and down on the waves.

"We shall be going down there, and thence sail into the mountain," explained the Pilgrim. "I rather think you will enjoy that voyage and especially what is to follow afterwards."

From the far end of the terrace a young girl approached, carrying a tray that she set down on our table. She placed four empty goblets and plates in front of us – cutlery, too. No food, however.

"Now you must decide for yourselves what you wish to eat!" Aranis urged us. "And, 'Hey Presto!' the food you desire will appear before you."

"Can't you 'Abracadabra' something for me?" I pleaded. "Best of all, I'd like to try some local specialty from this area of Sirius." Lydia eagerly nodded in agreement. Lissa was snoring loudly at her feet.

Barely a minute later, lovely, piping hot portions of food materialized before us. There were vegetable dishes with vegetables I didn't recognize, and in the center of the table was a long, freshly-baked loaf of bread that we could tear pieces off of. Despite Lydia's prior denial of hunger, she practically threw herself over the food and ate with a hearty appetite until all the dishes were quite clean. What a funny little thing my Angel friend is!

After we had eaten, Aranis led us to the wall behind the dining table. We hadn't noticed there was an elevator there. As we were stepping into the elevator, I wondered whether it had first been invented by us or the Sirians. This thought was interrupted by a brusque laugh.

"Actually it was here on Sirius," said Aranis. "Elevators have been in existence here for thousands of years; since the planet is so mountainous, the people needed a way to get up and down. The first elevators were a simple, open construction, but over the years they've developed into something more like the ones on Earth. Sirians have visited Earth many times and both learned and taught things – but mostly taught, of course!"

I held my tongue; he was probably right. The elevator stopped and we stepped out, with Lissa taking the lead. We came straight out into the harbor. That was in itself a great experience, with all those peculiar boats in every imaginable color and design. Aranis, closely followed by the Pilgrim and Lissa, stopped when reaching a boat in various shades of red and pink, with a silver dolphin figurehead at the prow. Almost immediately a ladder was thrown down, which affixed itself to the pier. All that remained was to go aboard.

The boat immediately glided away, leaving the land behind us. With a full sail of shimmering silver, we maintained a wonderfully steady speed. Fairly close to our left side loomed the high, dark cliff, emitting its strangely vibrant light. Someone started singing. It turned out to be a man, standing by the guard railing at the stern, who was singing the loveliest song. It was so beautiful that it brought tears to my eyes, and I noticed Lydia dabbing hers dry. Neither the music nor the song was like anything we are familiar with on Earth, but a singing voice is always a singing voice, even if this particular man's tones fluctuated between bass and tenor in a most unusual manner. As the song ended, the boat docked. The gangway was lowered and our two guides beckoned us to follow them.

We found ourselves in a cavity inside the cliff, where a wide ledge followed around the edge. We alighted onto a stairway, leading to the ledge. Down beneath us the azure water splashed, and we saw our boat gliding back out into the late sunshine, just starting to pale in the evening breeze. The cliff ledge led us on to a door in the rock, which opened up as we neared it. We remained standing in the doorway, petrified in awe of the delightful sight we beheld.

22. Evensong in the Ivory Cave

Why do I say, "Petrified in awe?"

It was simply stupendous! Somehow the enormity of it all was so shatteringly overwhelming and wondrous! The cavern auditorium was as though taken straight out of a science fiction book, illuminated as it was with a turquoise light, stemming from a large opening in the ceiling. Soothing and beautiful music filled our ears, but it took a while for our eyes to acclimatize to the light. There was a podium positioned centrally on the one long side, and the entire room was full of benches fixed to the floor. The benches were covered with soft cushions, but there were no backrests; they appeared to be just carved straight out of the rock.

We caught a glimpse of some light entities, appearing like a strange mist moving in some sort of fairy frolic along all sides of the room. The auditorium was not square – in fact nothing seemed square – for the one end was unevenly rounded and covered with growing plants, like a curtain. Exquisite aromas wafted out from there, like a thin veil of smoke.

Aranis and the Pilgrim hurried in between the rows of benches and sat down near the podium. Lydia and I followed suit. It wasn't exactly uncomfortable, but neither was it comfortable, sitting there without any back support. However, we soon had other things to occupy our minds.

Folks streamed in and, to my utmost surprise, the gigantic auditorium was swiftly not only filled, but also absolutely jam-packed. The room was chiefly filled with a variety of people, some very Earth-human-like, others amphibians, and there were those beings somewhat difficult to conclusively define. The light in the auditorium became more powerful, the music, too. The last members of the audience were squeezed in and then the doors were shut with a loud bang. The light dimmed again gradually and everyone stood straight up to attention in absolute silence, directing their unerring gaze at the podium, upon which a lady and a gentleman suddenly stood.

The lady had a pale green aura of light. She was incredibly beautiful, with a head of thick, silver-shimmering hair, crowned with a sparkling diadem. She had large, dark eyes, a well-formed little nose, and an attractively outlined mouth. As she smiled gently, one felt that her mouth radiated an all-encompassing Love that penetrated us all. The dress she wore sparkled as brilliantly as her diadem, and she held her arms outstretched towards the audience. This strangely gave us the sensation that we actually were being physically embraced. Apparently everyone in our company had felt this embrace physically, so I learned afterwards.

The gentleman was tall and his whole figure was shimmering gold. The top of the woman's head reached just up to his shoulders, which clearly marked how very tall he was, and his shoulder-length hair was in nuances of brown and gold. He had strong, attractive features and a magnificent smile. The cloak he wore made him look just like a golden statue – although a veritably animate one. When he stretched out his hands in greeting, we could actually feel his vibrating, physical handshake in our hands and his eyes looking deep into ours. This in itself was a most singular experience.

Then a voice was heard speaking. Every single word penetrated like some living entity into the ear, and finally embedded itself into the heart, where it was memorized forever. I have encountered many strange things, but never experienced anything quite like this. The words spoken were these:

"Welcome to the Sirius Evensong one and all – both you who are resident here, and those who have come from other celestial bodies! The song now vibrating in your hearts is a reverberation of the planet Sirius' own lyre. We are now in direct contact and coalescing with the One, the Mother/Father in our world and all other worlds resembling ours. There is an energy stream which will be directly transmitted between those of us present in Sirius' cavern auditorium and God who is the Creator and First Source. When the Primeval tone sounds, you will all become physical parts of Him/Her, of his/her Spirit and Emanation. Each and every one of you is ME!"

That which followed I shall never forget, being so much an Angel! Lydia concurs with me. Even Lissa sat absolutely still, seemingly in a state of sleep and waking both at once.

The problem lies in recounting it. Mariana, who was not actually present, has only my own account as reference, landing her with a somewhat difficult task. It was a cosmic experience, so far removed from anything Earthly that no words can accurately describe it. Perhaps it will suffice for you, the reader, if I say that the words and music flowed together in energies, which felt like warm threads enfolding our hearts and permeating them with an indescribable sense of extreme happiness. It was a sensation of perfect bliss which was felt from head to toe, radiating out into the arms and legs, making the heart feel it was literally expanding, warm and vibrating and filled with glittering, caressing, and transcendental golden rays. We may be blessed with a seemingly rich language, but it proves sadly limiting when I attempt giving justice to this overwhelming experience. The Evensong came with a light and a hymn that just happened. It happened to us all; we were smitten as with an embrace, a proof of Love – a Love that is boundless and infinite.

Suddenly, as though commanded, all in the room stood up. Only we remained seated, as Aranis had signaled us to do. Then we heard something – barely audible at first, like a low humming that gradually rose to a crescendo of vibrant jungle echoes that filled the great auditorium, the fullness and power of which cannot be described. A hymn of sheer joy, sung by a thousand-voiced choir, filled one's entire body, a joy and happiness whose counterpart just does not exist on the Earthly plane. The infinite Love was living in every single atom, in every single cell and in every single breath of the chanting air. The wordless hymn by beings from various planets combined in a melody of the spheres – an almighty and glorious symphony of Love.

We fell asleep embraced in Love. Sitting on our backless stone bench, we experienced the greatest fellowship in Space: the Love between all

127

created in the Cosmos. "It really is possible to Love everyone and everything," it rejoiced within me. "There are no limits."

Lydia turned around and gave me a look with infinity in her eyes. It was wonderful. It was fabulous. It was the most incredible Truth I had ever encountered, both as a human being and as an Angel. The Anthem of Truth resounded right through me; it penetrated every atom and every bit of every dimension I was aware of. It was Life itself singing to me – and for us all. It was the very essence of LIFE created by First Source that had been intended to give limitless beauty to the Creation.

What else is there to tell? The moment of Creation flowed through our hands and out into our bodies. The music of the spheres resounded in our ears and cosmic beauty dazzled our eyes.

Can one experience anything greater?

No, there cannot be anything more wonderful than to take part in Life's symphony of First Source.

Half-consciously, like sleepwalkers, we left this incredible, musically resounding auditorium.

The daylight brightness outside gave us a bit of a shock. I staggered around like a drunkard, noticing Lydia's predicament was the same and that the Pilgrim helpfully took hold of her hand to support her. It seemed to me that we stepped from one life to another and that the current one, the path we trod from the cave to the boats, was the less important of them. To discuss the continued part of the journey felt like an anti-climax – but necessary all the same.

We sat in one of the boats, feeling numbed by the overwhelming experience we'd had in the cavern auditorium, and listened to the boatman's gentle humming. Both Aranis and the Pilgrim kept silent, as though they had no wish to encroach upon the privacy of our numbness. Lissa crept underneath her master's seat to quietly curl up, since even she seemed to understand the greatness of all that we had undergone. It wasn't until we arrived at the harbor and once again stood on terra firma that our tongues finally loosened. Lydia and I profusely thanked our hosts and guides for the incredibly splendid Evensong. Then it was just a case of ascertaining where we were to go from there. Night had already fallen, and the dark violet lights in the harbor, together with the blazing, flickering lanterns of the boats, presented a most befitting ending to our adventure. But, sadly, we were then forced to move on.

"You are most welcome to spend the night with me in Agartha," invited the Pilgrim. "You may also stay here overnight, but that will entail a longer journey for you tomorrow. You have to travel back to the Pleiades, since your visit there was incomplete. However, as long as you are physical beings in human bodies, you need to sleep periodically. Take your farewell of Aranis, and then we must jump to!"

"I do so wonder who the couple commencing the ceremony in the cavern auditorium was?" was the question put by Lydia, of course.

"They were the supreme souls of Sirius, the ones who govern the planet with gentle, loving hands via direct confluence with First Source," replied Aranis gravely.

"It's going to be so hard leaving this planet," I sighed. "We are quite overcome."

"I feel so at home here," Lydia added in agreement. Both of us embraced our newly found friend, whom Mariana had known for so many years.

"You will always be most welcome to return," was the last we heard before the Pilgrim's grip on us both took us back to Earth at the speed of thought.

23. Pleiadean Journey to the Sister of Earth

We soon found ourselves plodding through the moss outside the Pilgrim's cave, and it felt comfortable. Once inside, we immediately fell sound asleep, exhausted after all the sensorial experiences of the day. It wasn't until breakfast the next morning that I was in a fit state of mind to concentrate on hearing our host's further plans for us.

"The Pleiades comprise not only the star Electra, that you visited," he announced, "the Pleiadean Star League is similar to your ..."

"... United Nations!" interrupted Lydia, finishing his sentence for him. The Pilgrim nodded in assent.

"Yes, something like that," he responded. "The Pleiades are composed of many highly developed Galactic Societies that jointly form an unparalleled star cluster. Clearly the seven brightest stars in this cluster are Alcyone, Merope, Sterope, Maia, Tageta, Celaeno, and Electra, where you were. There are more than 250,000 stars pertaining to this star cluster. In all, 200 planetary systems (star nations) have united to form the Pleiadean Star League, situated somewhere between 200 and 500 light years away from planet Earth.

"The indigenous peoples on the Pleiades descend from Andromeda and Lyra. They dedicate themselves to the study of spiritual arts and science. One could say that art and natural logic expresses their humanity. It is this that the two of you now are to make a closer study of. You are to ascertain the various levels and give an account of their influence on the rest of the Universe."

"Phew!" I groaned, as I took a ladleful of the exceedingly good soup the Pilgrim had set out on the stone table, "That's quite a task!"

"May we go home afterwards?" Lydia piped up, while rubbing Lissa's fur. "I am so enamored with this gorgeous doggy that I really don't ever want to leave her. Will you come with us, Pilgrim?"

"I will transport you there," replied the Pilgrim with a smile. "We shall see whether I can remain there a while. This time we're going to Alcyone. I suppose I shall just have to continue acting as your guide. Now we'll go for a little walk."

We followed after the Pilgrim and his dog, through a woodland path that was so mossy and adorned with flowers that it reminded me of the ones back home in Södermanland or Dalecarlia. (Dalecarlia was an addendum made by Mariana, who joined us on this journey!) I inhaled the aromas of pine, birch, moss, and ripe berries. I didn't recognize the berries, but they were similar to large bilberries, the green leaves of which were also bigger.

A deafening roar caused both Lydia and I to suddenly stop in our tracks. The Pilgrim giggled. "Just like all waterfalls, this one is a bit raucous!" he teased.

The woodland path opened out into a grove, and then the raucous waterfall revealed itself in all its glory. It appeared to tumble down out of nowhere high above, and the cascading water glimmered, shimmered, and danced playfully with a wild force. It was wider than Niagara Falls; I couldn't see the other side. All was tempestuous water – frothing, foaming waves and soaring, multi-colored droplets. Lydia stood with her hand on Lissa's head and just beheld the view. Both of them just observed.

The Pilgrim placed his hand on my shoulder. "Now you have seen the most beautiful waterfall in the world!" he yelled, in an attempt to override the loud crashing noise of the water. "Stand closer to me, so we can commence our next journey!"

He placed his arms around us, and Lissa tucked herself in between his legs. We somehow managed to capture a split second of non-existent time, that otherwise persistently eludes us. We closed our eyes to the musical din of the waterfall and re-opened them to the very same tones, only much fainter. We were still standing by a waterfall, but this one was much smaller and not quite so very blue.

"Welcome to Alcyone, which could be the sister of Earth!" The Pilgrim made a sweeping gesture with his hand, indicating the rather pretty, though fairly ordinary, scene of a waterfall, behind which loomed tall pines, moss-covered mountains, and cliffs. From where we were standing on the riverbank, we could see that between us and the friendly waterfall was a rather ordinary fence, apparently made out of iron wire. The waterfall rumbled, but nowhere near as loudly as the previous one. However, upon closer inspection as I bent over the fence, I was confronted with something new to me: In the middle of the bouncing contortions of the waterfall glowed slender, shimmering bodies. These were in fact Undines – water spirits – who were dancing in the froth of the waterfall.

Their bodies looked quite transparent, but probably it was the effect of the water that projected this illusory image. One water spirit stretched out its arms in a swimming motion; it was so close to me that I could clearly see he had proper little arms and a proper body, very like a human's, only very much smaller. We had arrived at a planet where the Elementals dared to show themselves. In a tall pine tree, behind the Pilgrim, I could see a mischievous faun cheerfully waving. A little farther away, centaurs were galloping around, racing one another. We noticed a sleepy little boy troll lying in the moss, as we turned around to take the woodland path leading away. Lydia's merry laugh rang out as she lifted her long dress to avoid treading on him.

"The Nature of Alcyone is very like the Earth's, but one of the greatest differences is that what Earth regards as 'Fairy-tale Creatures' are here commonly encountered, veritably real beings. They symbiotically live with people, as do the animals here. There are no hunters; the people and animals leave one another alone to live in perfect peace. To eat meat is also unthinkable; all life forms are vegetarian. I personally consider this to be a true Paradise. I sometimes like to wander around here, but there is nothing that requires any help from me, so Lissa and I always have to return to Earth, where there is great need of our help."

"So what are we doing here, then?" I wondered.

"For the same reason I accompanied you," smiled the Pilgrim,

"I wanted to show you the Kingdom of Peace, so that you can give your report about this, too. Even the climate here is pleasant over the whole planet, which adds to the welfare and the sense of well-being. In contrast to Earth, Alcyone is a light and friendly planet. The inhabitants of Alcyone have come as far as they need with their inventions, without having disrupted what Nature intended for plants and wildlife. Pan adores this planet and is a frequent visitor here."

"Do they believe in God here, too?" inquired Lydia, ceaselessly interested in all the Pilgrim had to say.

"I shall show you one of their 'churches,' so you can see for yourself" replied the Pilgrim.

We had just come out of the wood, and before us lay what I can only describe as a little village. We could see a number of small, low-built houses. All the houses were overgrown with flowering plants, had mossy roofs and many windows – in fact reminiscent of the more primitive style of summer cottages commonly built in Sweden in the early twentieth century, although the latter naturally lacked the many windows. At first glimpse one hadn't an inkling of how they were anything but primitive.

"Let's go in!" declared the Pilgrim, simply walking straight in. We followed in closely behind him, then halted and just stared. Five people were sitting at a crudely carved wooden table, eating something that looked like speckled porridge or a dish of some sort of grain with spices. There was a man, a woman holding a baby, and also a boy and a girl somewhere between the ages of seven to ten years old. The man stood up as we entered; upon seeing the Pilgrim he embraced him warmly. As usual, we were able to understand the local language of the planet spoken.

"Welcome, dear Pilgrim," said the short, stocky man heartily, who might easily have been a Swedish farmer. He certainly didn't look much like an alien from Outer Space. Three cats were sitting in a row on one of the windowsills. They looked slightly different from our cats – these ones had both longer tails and ears, and two of the cats were larger than their cousins on Earth, while the third was rather smaller. All three were mottled amber.

"I think I must be back home in England!" whispered Lydia.

"... or Sweden," I whispered back, grinning.

The people were like us, with houses like ours – even the cats were like ours (well almost). We truly felt at home. However, I didn't spot any Earthly electrical kitchen appliances, despite the food appearing to be piping hot. In fact, there was no cooker, oven, or fireplace of any kind to be seen. The Pilgrim obviously noticed our bewilderment as we courteously smiled and nodded to all at the table. The smallest cat jumped down from the windowsill and sneaked up close to both Lydia and Lissa. The dog gave the cat a little lick with its pink tongue.

"How do you cook your food?" asked Lydia, unable to refrain from posing the question. All of a sudden three empty chairs appeared at the table for us to sit on. Just then the lady of the house opened her mouth to speak, while wiping the baby's face.

"Cook food?" she echoed quizzically. "We simply create our food and then we eat it. Created food is eaten all over the planet. We create it ourselves, as we are taught from the very beginning. It sounds to me as though you come from that barbaric planet, Earth!"

The young farmer's wife gave a little laugh. She was very pretty, with fair, wavy hair sticking out from under a white bonnet, and wore a most becoming, floral frock. She laid the baby down in the cradle that was standing next to her and then set a food pot on the table, containing the same sort of grain dish the family had been eating. Plates, glasses, and cutlery appeared at once, wherever they had been conjured up from. We politely sampled a little of the porridge – then we took a little more, and finally ate it all up. It was absolutely delicious; I'd never tasted any porridge like this before! Delicious just wasn't the word – it tasted heavenly (although up there nothing tastes of anything, of course). I don't think I've ever eaten anything quite as good, and Lydia said the same. It just seemed to melt in your mouth and left an exquisite aftertaste that was the best of all ... it's just impossible to do it justice with the meager words I have to express. The fact that we were able to enjoy the food to such an extent confirmed that we were in our ordinary, physical bodies.

"You wished to visit our church," said the farmer, with a jolly laugh. "Well, you're doing that right now. Our home is our church. We also have buildings in which all who live here occasionally congregate. We do hold meetings, either to discuss or decide our thoughts regarding certain community quandaries, or simply for social gatherings with music, dancing, and singing. Such meetings are frequently held in the Village Hall, which I can show you, if you wish. But since there is only one God, and he/she is the same for all inhabitants of this planet, no actual church is necessary. God exists as much within us as without; it's really as simple as that, don't you think?"

I felt a little embarrassed when I reflected on the multitude of deviant faiths and religions practiced on Earth. It was quite unnecessary and a ridiculous source of trouble and strife. Wouldn't the Earth be a far better place with so much more Love, if only this same reasoning was applied there? I looked at Lydia and could see she had drawn approximately the same conclusion.

"Profuse thanks to you for your kind offer of showing us the Village Hall," I said, "but we'd much rather see a little more of Nature and the beings who dwell therein. I happened to catch a glimpse of one of the Elementals over by the river, when we arrived here."

"They lead concurrent lives with us and are the very best of neighbors to have," said the farmer, whose name was Ejur. His wife was called Nia. "They can tell stories, for all children adore fairy-tales," he continued.

"It is with great regret that we have to travel on!" interjected the Pilgrim.

I should have liked nothing better than to tarry, but the Pilgrim knew what lay ahead of us, and we trusted his decision. We took our farewells of the hospitable farming family and set off for the woods. Ejur and Nia emphasized that we were most welcome back to see them before leaving the planet. "It surely isn't exactly the same everywhere?" Lydia asked our friend.

"The family you've just met is typical of the inhabitants on Alcyone," responded the Pilgrim. "There are no large towns or cities here, just many, many little villages, very like the one we've just been to. They are by no means identical, but there's not much to set them apart."

With that we were content to plunge ourselves into the depths of the whispering, humming shadows of the wood, as the evening tiptoed in.

24. Night at the Pleiades

Lydia took my hand. It was eerie in the woods; it rustled and the wind blew, there were sighs and whispering to be heard. The Pilgrim stood still. He took out a little whistle, which sounded a signal, resulting in a hissing noise coming out from behind us. A well-lit vehicle came to a halt with a sliding sound.

"I think it might be better if we continue our journey in this," advised our friend, and blew another signal with his whistle. A door opened and a ladder was hoisted down. All that remained was to step into the vehicle, which was much like the previous ones we'd travelled in, i.e., oblong with round edges, a place at the front where the Pilgrim and Lissa sat, plus two seats behind for Lydia and me. It felt safer than the forest.

We were lifted up high above the treetops. Once we slowly and steadily glided onwards, through a veil of clouds like airy cobwebs above us, the Pilgrim announced, "I would like to tell you where we are heading to. This planet has two sides to it, and we are now on our way to the other side. It isn't at all like the place we have just left behind; this place is more of a rough wilderness, with the sea, jagged cliffs, and dark forests."

"There was a forest where we embarked," Lydia corrected him.

"Quite right, my dear," retorted the Pilgrim, "only that was a well-tended forest in which the Elementals dwell. Conversely, the forest we are about to visit is not well tended, and those who dwell there are somewhat primitive. The inhabitants are known as the Xelurers, a people quite different from any other you have met; but they are actually human beings, with a culture entirely their own. They are bellicose and extremely wary of strangers. I know them and have been accepted by them, so therefore I advise that you stick very close to me to ensure no harm will befall you. Lissa has been there before and will be prepared to defend you, should we be attacked."

"That sounds ghastly!" I protested.

"Not really, but I fancy it could be a rather interesting experience for you to give an account of to those up above, from whence you've come," assured the Pilgrim with a little smile. "Of course, nothing perilous will happen to you; I simply wanted to prepare you for what may be expected."

"Thanks a lot. I'll be sticking to Lissa like glue." No mistaking who responded with that statement!

The vehicle landed with a muffled thud. We peered out of the windows, viewing only mountains as far as the eye could see. There was neither road nor forest in sight, only a mass of cliffs of various heights. It looked dark and ominous.

"It's early morning here," the Pilgrim informed us, as we stood on the jagged rock, shivering with cold. He hastily apologized, immediately conjuring up long, fur-lined coats and comfortable, little, fur-lined boots – the latter made one feel as though walking on cushions with wonderfully supportive soles. In the next instant we were equipped with appropriate leather mittens and bonnets. I could tell by Lydia's amused expression that I must have looked like an enormous teddy bear, but then the Pilgrim didn't look much better either. Lissa sat down on the cliff, stared at us, and barked. Not even Lydia was her usual, gracious self – she looked remarkably like a giant rat. Outfitted in this manner, we stomped our way straight into the thick of the mountains, keeping close to the Pilgrim. Our vehicle remained where we had left it.

We walked across the coarse moss in the bitter cold, as I once in an earlier life had been accustomed; only here there was no snow or ice, just a nasty dampness that the ground exuded, like an evil-smelling steam rising from a cooking pot. The stench was nauseating, but since the Pilgrim doggedly plowed on with Lissa, we dutifully followed in their footsteps. We then left the ledge of the cliff and went straight into a labyrinth of upright stones that stood taller than us.

It soon became clear to us why such a labyrinth was positioned at that particular point, for out of the blue, a mass of natives came running from behind us. I say "natives," because I don't know how else to describe them. They had lightly tanned skin and bodies that looked entirely human. The majority of them were masked, but those who weren't had enormous dark eyes, sharp, beak-like noses, and long, drooping ears. Their mouths were large, but otherwise difficult to describe, since they were yelling at us – or presumably yelling, to be exact, because we couldn't hear a sound.

"The Xelurers communicate solely telepathically; they do not speak, for they are totally mute," explained the Pilgrim. "One has to learn how to read their facial expressions, if one lives here. Should you happen to misread anyone, you'll soon know about it." He gave out a burst of laughter.

At that moment a Xelurer stood right in front of him, and there was no doubt about his intimidating glare. I was about to take hold of Lydia's hand, but suddenly realized she had disappeared; Lissa was sitting where she ought to have stood and it was hardly surprising to see that the dog was confused.

"Where is Lydia?" I asked the Pilgrim, who was engaged in a very loud discussion with the intimidator, in which only one voice was heard.

"She'll be back shortly," he replied. "Apparently the women of this village wish to take a closer look at her. They are not used to having visitors here."

Not being able to see Lydia or know where she was felt uncomfortably strange to me. We had kept one another company the whole time. I shot a glance at the Pilgrim and he gave me a reassuring smile.

"I think I must now fetch Lydia back," I announced sharply, while trying to elbow my way past the Xelurers, which was not at all easy. They stood formed like a compact pillar, impeding my way through the gap in the rock that I was aiming for. When I tried to pass them I was met with a great deal of resistance.

The Pilgrim grabbed hold of me. "Please do not attempt anything further, my dear Jan, for it may become fearfully unpleasant. Just stand as close to me as you possibly can. Lissa will sense any imminent danger and convey this to me in her own way." He spoke a few more words to the leader of the Xelurers and then beckoned to me to accompany him with this man.

"He will take us to Lydia," explained my friend soothingly. "Come along now!" Lissa pressed herself closely against her master's legs and I took hold of his arm in order to squeeze myself past the Xelurer standing nearest me, who menacingly checked every move I made. A concentrated odor of sweat and some sort of herbal, aromatic fat encircled me. This was definitely not the most pleasant area of the Pleiades. I began to wonder if there were more unpleasantries existing in any other places within this huge star cluster, or for that matter in the entire Universe.

The Pilgrim read my thoughts. "Would you call it 'unpleasantries,' Janne?" he teased. "I'd sooner call it caution founded on experience. Once upon a time this area underwent unfathomable hardship. In those days the star wars were in full force, that nowadays, thankfully, have virtually ceased to exist in this Universe (on Earth a film has been made about this that may be seen at the cinema!). Almost the entire species was wiped out, so only a few Xelurers escaped their near extinction by successfully hiding themselves. This handful of survivors was the ancestral root of the new people who, quite understandably, have an inherent mistrust of anything remotely alien to them. It is our hope that this intrinsically suspicious characteristic will soon be dispelled, becoming a thing of the past, for it is not representative of the Pleiades in general."

By edging our way around the cliffs via roads only locally known, we eventually arrived at an open area, which appeared to be part of a household. Lissa barked and rushed over to Lydia, who was sitting in a corner of the cliff, surrounded by Xelurian women. These ladies formed a compact wall all around her, but they immediately made way for the bounding dog to run through, enabling Lissa to jump up on Lydia and lay her paws upon her shoulders. Lydia had looked despondent, but lit up the instant the Pilgrim's dog zoomed up to her. The womenfolk immediately closed in on Lydia again, so as to block her off once more.

They were not too successful in this, however, since long before we were able to come to the rescue, Lissa had revealed an aggressive side to her nature, with threateningly poised head and bared teeth, loudly growling a serious warning.

The Pilgrim and I led Lydia out between us towards the road back. They were evidently not used to dogs, for these grim warriors, who earlier acted so threateningly, swiftly withdrew into the background.

We partly dragged and partly carried Lydia all the way back to our vehicle. When she finally sank into her seat, she leaned back and gave a huge sigh.

"I never thought I was going to get away from there alive," she groaned. "They pushed and pulled at me as though I were a piece of dough being kneaded. I really believed they were going to kill me; their facial expressions were really ghastly – and I couldn't even talk to them. Please take us away from this horrid place!"

And without any more ado, we left.

25. Next Stop: Andromeda

Lydia perked up during the return journey, so that when we finally stopped outside the Pilgrim's cave on our dear Mother Earth, her tears started to flow.

"How silly I've been!" she sobbed. "All the time I knew you were close at hand and no harm could come to me. I am after all an Angel – although back there I just felt like a defenseless little girl from Earth who'd landed herself in trouble. I am so sorry!"

The Pilgrim smiled kindly and set a pot of water over the fire. I gave my colleague a big hug and gave vent to a burst of laughter.

"Well that's the end of that short and sweet journey!" I lamented. "So what are we to do now?"

"Hold a meeting," suggested our friend, setting out mugs of piping hot tea and a plate of newly-baked bread out of nowhere – besides cheese, butter, and a wonderful selection of fresh vegetables. With healthy appetites we devoured the inviting fare provided, since our bodies still were in their physical state.

After we had finished eating, we relaxed in the comfortable armchairs in the Pilgrim's far from meager living room. One might easily imagine that a Pilgrim shunned all worldly luxuries, but you'd be quite wrong regarding this particular one! Consequently, I suspected that our Pilgrim might very well belong to the Great White Brotherhood, which I was determined to ascertain.

"What a lovely place you have!" I declared vigilantly. "Have you always lived here?"

"No," he replied cagily, with a smirk. "Would you like a biscuit with your coffee, Lydia?" he divergently inquired. She emphatically nodded with delight, and in an instant a plate filled with the most delicious biscuits stood on the table. But I was not going to be thwarted, being in my most obstinate of moods.

"Won't you tell us who you really are, before we travel on?" I persisted. "I have a feeling you are one of the Masters, but which one of them?"

"Perhaps not the one you think," he cryptically replied. "I shall divulge the answer to your question when the time is right. Till then you will just have to take me at face value for the Pilgrim I am. Incidentally, it may interest you to know that I will continue assisting you on the rest of your journey – and the next destination is the Andromedan Confederacy."

"No, really?" shrieked Lydia, "Are we going all the way there? To Andromeda? Will we be allowed in there?"

"And why shouldn't we be?" I snapped. "I have dreamt of Andromeda since I was a little boy. There were few nights I didn't look out from the kitchen bench in my childhood home, gaining comfort from the stars, as I gazed at them in their proper positions in the immense Universe."

"Well, you now will be able to see all of them from within the planets themselves!" smirked the Pilgrim. "Perhaps it will soon be revealed that the inside of your own planet is inhabited."

I stared at him, utterly horrified. "You surely can't mean that? Would that change the attitudes of Earth humans?"

"That would be good," commented Lydia dryly. "Then there might not be so much conflict; they are always fighting all over the place – if not with the armed forces, then at least verbally."

"We shall see what you think of Andromeda," responded the Pilgrim. "I think Janne is likely to change his opinion."

And I certainly did.

I lived on Earth until 1968, by which time I had become an old man. What later happened to my beloved Earth I learned only through accounts given by others. As far as I was concerned, my finest memories of life on Earth pertained to the flora and fauna. That these two concepts could be utilized in the Inner Earth would have been the farthest thing from my mind before visiting Agartha. I then understood why humans on Earth so doggedly refused to believe there were any inhabited planets other than their own. It was too difficult to envision an inhabited, flourishing part of our Earth on its inside. I remembered I had read General Byrd's account of Agartha and people had, at the time, dismissed it as the wild imaginings of an old, weak-brained man. Was there any chance at all of my knowledge and evidence ever managing to reach Earth, apart from with this book? That remained to be seen.

We took a little walk to the beautiful waterfall. I believe it was in that very spot I experienced the rather vague, but nevertheless genuine, perception of how infinite we are and the magnitude of our mission, making me feel like a tiny ant that had been caught up in a whirlwind, but whose fragile wings would soon carry him to freedom in the air.

Up we went and down we came. That waterfall was certainly enchanted, and I welcomed its magic. It had transformed itself into a different, new waterfall – and the Pilgrim had vanished. Lydia and I stood holding one another, down beneath the raging tumbling of clear, glistening water. Or perhaps I should say, held on to one another, for the quaking of the ground created such a vibrant din that it was impossible to make oneself heard. I turned around slowly. We were standing on a shiny, white marble ledge with a firm, gilt railing. "Lissa has disappeared," wailed Lydia, drying a tear away from her cheek.

"You'll soon see her again," I consoled. "The Pilgrim will certainly come to collect us when it is time. Have you forgotten we are here to explore a new planet? Come now, it's going to be fun!"

We caught hold of one another's hands and stepped gingerly down the marble stairway. It was wet and slippery, but there were man-made, gilt banisters to hold on to on both sides, all the way down. Beneath us green and bluish treetops glistened. The stairway was rather long and curved gently down to the left.

Finally we reached the ground, which appeared to be covered with white gravel. There were tall flowerpots standing in a row below, containing plants in warm red and mauve colors. There were some white benches to rest on, and I discovered we had come down to a circular plateau. Surrounding it was a forest, similar to a Swedish one. Yet again! We followed our Swedish forest over many different planets – or was it perhaps we who brought the forest with us? Had the Pilgrim been playing a practical joke and sent us to some remote place in the USA? Perhaps we were back home on the surface!

Andromeda! The name alone was so enchanting, I thought. We sat on one of the benches awhile, before continuing onwards. I had to consider which way we were to go.

"Oh, it doesn't really matter, does it?" giggled Lydia. "There must be some people living around here somewhere who we can ask." She stood up and held her arms under the water flowing from above and continued to laugh in an escalating pitch, until she ended up screaming. Then she jumped back, pretty well soaked through. I conjured up a towel out of the air – we had learned how to do this sort of thing ages ago.

Lydia had barely managed to finish drying herself when a woman suddenly stood beside us, without either of us having the faintest idea where she had come from. She was fairly tall, with fair, artistically plaited hair, large violet eyes, and a generous mouth. She was dressed in something akin to national costume: a long, colorfully patterned, full skirt, with a white blouse covered by a plain red bodice, and a dainty little embroidered bonnet on her head. I was wracking my brains for a description and could only come up with "dirndl," but that wasn't really right.

"Hello!" said the woman unceremoniously – or rather a girl. As usual, we understood what she said perfectly. "I wish to welcome you and am here to initially take care of you. Come with me!" She spun around on her heels, walked through the narrow opening between the benches and turned her head. "I know your names are Jan and Lydia," she called out. "Mine is Kyranina Lilia, but you may call me Kyra. First, I'll take you to my home."

She walked very quickly, causing her hips to lightly sway. Her feet hardly touched the ground, so we had difficulty keeping up with her. Then, all of a sudden, she came to halt. We just about managed to see we were in a forest. It was quite an ordinary forest, just like any other. We had reached a little opening amidst the trees, and there stood a carriage. The carriage had no wheels, just something that looked a bit like the runners of a sledge. There were four seats inside. We hopped in. Right at the front was a dashboard, which the girl pressed at. The carriage immediately started up, more like a quiet car than our earlier modes of transport throughout the planets. A well-maintained pathway meandered ahead of us, with the forest to one side and a river on the other that presumably the waterfall flowed into.

"There are no towns here. I believe them to be a peculiarity to Earth, where people seem to live like ants in an anthill. We find that dreadful. We are all very much individuals here, even though we all are part of a higher consciousness. Our culture instills this in us, whether through singing, dancing, playing, writing, or painting, etc. I've heard that your culture is sadly lacking, and that is why you are here to learn from us, is that correct?"

I just nodded. This conversation, if one could call it that, was not to my taste, but just then Lydia interrupted our young babbler, "You said that you as individuals are part of a higher consciousness. What exactly do you mean by that?"

"You'll have to talk to Father or Mother about that; I have to dash off to the swimming pool with my little brother as soon as I reach home, and we'll be arriving there in just a moment."

The carriage stopped outside an extremely ornate, high gate. We climbed out while Kyra fiddled about on the dashboard, setting it to automatically return from whence it had come. We opened the gate and stepped into a most beautiful garden, although this was far from the first beautiful garden I'd encountered in so many places before. I came to think especially of the hanging terraced gardens on Sirius. Surely nothing more astoundingly beautiful in the way of gardens could possibly exist? Although after we had gone a little farther, I began to wonder!

I regret I do not know the names of all the flowers that grew so prolifically, bordering the white gravel path. However, they created a glorious burst of color beyond compare, causing Lydia and I to stop in our tracks, totally enraptured by the wondrous floral gaiety. Kyra turned around with a look of impatience, so I tugged at Lydia's sleeve to drag her along with me.

"You can see more later," I whispered. "The girl seems annoyed that we've lingered."

We had arrived at a large door, framed by lovely, wonderfully aromatic vines. A man opened it, and we glimpsed a woman standing behind him. Kyra sneaked in and disappeared, having waved at us hastily.

Both the man and the woman looked completely humanlike, but this was no surprise, since the Pilgrim had already told us that Andromeda was chiefly inhabited by humans, barring a few of the annexing, smaller stars.

The couple was not content to simply shake our hands, but embraced both of us most heartily. It became increasingly apparent to me that the majority of inhabitants of the Milky Way planets were extremely kind and hospitable people.

I simply could not resist taking a step back to see what the door was mounted in. The house was white, made of some sort of semi-transparent stone or concrete, and looked roughly like an ordinary house on Earth: i.e., with four walls, a sparkling red roof, and flower-adorned veranda that faced towards the heavenly, gloriously adorned garden. The smiling couple really made us feel most welcome at once, and completely at home, too.

Our hostess was called Zoa and was an exact, older version of her daughter. Our host was called Ranira and looked like an Egyptian Prince. Zoa wore a similar "national costume" to her daughter's; Ranira wore a white, ruffled shirt and dark, tight-fitting breeches with long tassels. Both of them had shoes that looked rather like clogs, but were flatter and definitely not made of wood. The latter were decoratively painted with a floral design and looked extremely comfortable.

"Whenever we arrive at a new planet, we're always so hospitably received by couples such as yourselves," I enthused.

"That is because we have a very well-organized system of communication between the planets," replied Ranira. "We know precisely who we are to receive and the reasons for their visit. It would seem that it is possible on Earth for any Tom, Dick, or Harry to drop in and visit anyone at any time, making demands and causing all sorts of trouble. But if everyone converses with others within the worlds of Space, all concerned will know who the visitors are and the purpose of their stay. Within the planet we have a system similar to yours, but what I formerly spoke of concerns interplanetary guests. It is extremely tranquil over all Andromeda, and disturbances are very rare. Humans from Earth are not yet able to travel throughout the Cosmos – but such a time will come in the future. Your research is well on its way to perfecting galactic travel. But before this is achieved, the human beings on Earth must be disciplined and brought up properly!"

"Just think how little we have known on Earth," I sighed.

"And they haven't advanced since we left it," added Lydia. "They certainly don't like to rush things there!"

Everyone laughed and we followed our hosts into their house. It didn't need much dusting. I mean there were very few knick-knacks, and neither clocks nor lamps.

"Easily managed," was Lydia's laconic opinion.

Zoa giggled. "I know how it is on Earth," she said. "You jam-pack your homes with possessions. Some houses are like that here, too, but I don't want to live like that. We have precisely enough for our needs, and if we require anything more, we simply create it."

I looked down at my feet. I was wearing sandals and the floor felt pleasantly soft. It was carpeted with a number of lovely rugs in various beautiful colors. There were no curtains; the windows were bare, but attractively so, since they gave the rooms the appearance of being larger, and one had the full benefit of the bounteous garden outside. Furthermore, the window frames and mullions were beautifully carved and ornamented. It was apparent that plants pervaded everywhere, even inside the house – Lydia had not failed to notice this, either. There was no shortage of comfortable seating, however; these were covered in light fabrics that matched the walls. We didn't see any pictures or bookshelves, but one of the walls in the drawing room was like a screen for projecting films on. This constantly displayed alternating pictures in muted colors, mostly ones of plants, parks, or some other motif of

Nature or animals. A dog, a cat, and some other, indiscernible, smaller pet were on the sofa, scrutinizing us. Lydia, of course, rushed over to stroke and make a fuss over them, but they did not respond to her cooing and moved off.

There was no kitchen. Everything one wished for was "conjured up" there. Our hosts sat at a table with us and pronounced, "Please eat or drink whatever you wish – you only have to say what you'd like." Since we still had our physical bodies, we were rather hungry, but I've never been much of a cook and I found it difficult to think what to ask for. Lydia instantly saw my dilemma and, thankfully, came to my rescue by ordering two most delicious, individual vegetable pies, which immediately appeared before us. She then additionally wished for bread, butter, cheese, and coffee – which also materialized on the table. What an agreeable place to live in!

26. Andromedan Experiences

We ate and chatted to our hearts' content, and then our hosts offered to show us around. We were given to understand that we would be travelling in some sort of vehicle, and Zoa fetched one just like her daughter had transported us in, or perhaps it was the very same. She reiterated what Kyra already had told us, i.e., that it was not densely inhabited there, nor were there any towns or villages, but that everything was quite individual and set apart. There were no shops either, since the convenient art of creative precipitation made their services obsolete. There were, however, pathways to walk along, which we kept to all the time. These paths were incredibly well looked after and the borders were sheer works of art with their flowers and fences. We frequently passed over bridges that crossed streams or rivers, and the climate was comfortably warm. The sun was not relentlessly scorching, but shone down gently.

"Are we on the outside of the planet or its inside?" I queried.

"On the inside, of course," replied Ranira. "The outside is uninhabitable, just as the Earth's soon will be. You have destroyed your Earth, and this will soon become apparent. The inside of the Andromedan planets were actually already inhabited many thousands of years ago. In fact, all the inhabited planets within our Universe are populated on the inside. The outside is too troubled and vulnerable. We knew the Earth was making a grave error in colonizing the outside, but the Earthlings would not listen. They were ignorantly headstrong and must now pay the price. Now Agartha has the task of helping to sow some sense into your world."

"This I did not know!" I exclaimed.

"Your daughter mentioned that you all are individuals who are part of a higher consciousness," interrupted Lydia. "Would you please explain what that entails? Is it your religion?"

"We never mention that word," retorted Ranira emphatically. "That word divides people and causes rifts, schisms, and even wars. Our children haven't heard it uttered, and it is therefore banned from use. We are aware of the situation on Earth regarding this, even though the Master Jesus was sent there to alter the concept. He sadly succeeded only in founding something that developed into yet another religion, with the most horrific consequences. Here he is counted as one amongst the gentle and benevolent Masters and Helpers guiding us everywhere, to ensure that the Language of Love is spoken. This is the only mutually common language we all share, barring a few differences in dialect. We are now about to disembark."

The vehicle gently came to a halt and we stepped out in front of an extremely tall building – a skyscraper, but wider than they usually are. Lydia counted eleven stories, she later told us, which probably doesn't seem so very high to Earthlings. In fact, it wasn't at all like any skyscrapers on Earth; it was built of the same, glittery, translucent material as our hosts' house. I was about to ask what it was, when Ranira anticipated my question.

"If you're wondering what building material we use," he smilingly declared, "you won't find anything like it on Earth, for it is unique to Andromeda. However, we have shipped it out to other planets – for example, Sirius. It is a remarkable material in that plants seek it out. It is extremely easy to cultivate, which is why you see such a proliferation of blossoming plants on this planet. The material may be found everywhere; it's a sort of rock-composite that induces optimal growth of vegetation. It is for this reason that we have no weeds here – they veer away from this outstanding material. This Andromedan planet is sometimes referred to as the Flower Planet – so now you see why. We are to go into our Meeting House – come!"

Ranira and his wife hastened up the steep steps that led to the entrance of the skyscraper. Once inside, we stepped into an elevator, which consisted of a circular platform with a pole in the middle to hold on to. At first we were alarmingly startled when we reached the top, for we thought we were suspended in the air. Happily we soon discovered that we were standing and walking around in some sort of glass balloon, from which we had the most wonderful, panoramic view. Our hosts laughed heartily at seeing our unwarranted apprehension.

The view was hard to describe, but astoundingly beautiful. One might have expected to see a town below, but there were only a few small houses, surrounded by lovely gardens, dotted around here and there, in amongst the countryside. On the horizon lay a fairly large lake, with its rippling, glittering waves. We could see boats sailing around on it. From such a distance away they looked quite ordinary – with the exception of their sails, which were oddly positioned, and in jumbled colors.

We descended again with our hosts; a short, spiral staircase led to the floor beneath the glass, spectator terrace, where we were ushered into a large chamber with a stage at the back. It could have been a theater back home in Sweden, if it hadn't been for the rather peculiar decor.

"This is one of the conference rooms," explained Zoa. "There are several, both large and small. We jointly make decisions regarding most areas, and there are various clans who focus their specific skills into such things as culture, architecture, planning of roads, hospitals, etc."

"Hospitals!" exclaimed Lydia. "Are there such things on this planet? I thought you only had healers here."

"Naturally we must have somewhere to place the ailing who require treatment, in whatever form it takes. Sometimes more than one treatment may be necessary. The system we have is considered most satisfactory; grave illnesses such as cancer no longer exist here – we have managed to find cures and eliminate them all."

"What about educational institutions: schools?" I inquired.

Ranira gave a little laugh in response. "But of course we have schools to educate the young. All children are taught to read, write, and many other things. We have schools scattered all over the planet. No one is expected to have to travel very far to school; special transport is provided to collect and drop pupils off as required. The classes are kept manageably small, with a maximum of ten children in each; they learn so much better then. You won't see any books, because they are creatively conjured when required. There are books on all subjects, many just like on Earth, and others that we specifically conjure up. We also have computers, which are different than yours and are extremely simple to use."

"But do you think it's always positive that all is so easily accessible to the children?" asked Lydia. "Doesn't that make them lazy?"

Once again Ranira laughed in response. "Quite the contrary." He looked keenly at his wife. "Ask Zoa; she's a teacher!"

"Education is considerably stricter than you might imagine," Zoa smilingly clarified. "If you think we are lax in our methods, you would be wrong. We maintain a healthy authority over our children, but as yet you have not met many. We apply something seldom used by you, something our children here have in abundance from birth – namely Love. The most severe form of punishment we have is to verbally reason with a child, so that they are made to understand their folly. If this doesn't prove effective, then we have alternative methods, but always applied with Love."

"By being put to work at something, perhaps?" was my suggestion.

Zoa looked most perplexed. "But work isn't punishment, surely? All work here is a labor of Love. If a task is presented as interesting and fun, then that's precisely how it will be. The idea is to obliterate all that is negative. This is the basic principle which most planets – and in particular Andromeda and Sirius – take as their standpoint. The Earth has taken the wrong standpoint: The night darkness conceals Love's light. Perhaps we should move on, do you think? You have only very limited time here, my husband informs me; although we regard time as fairly flexible, the only timeframes we use are day, night, and when our stomachs cry out!"

"What about animals?" our animal-loving Lydia interjected. "I haven't seen any dogs, cats, or horses hereabouts."

"Then you haven't looked properly." Zoa laughed heartily. "Of course we have pets – and then there are wild animals in the woods and sea. The wild ones do not pose a threat, since we leave them in peace. The tame ones may be found all over the place, as pets or in a helping capacity. We do not kill animals for their skins or flesh, if that's what you meant. We let Nature take care of itself without interference from us. One could describe many places on this planet as one great big zoo! However, we only apply methods that will not harm the animals whenever we wish to adapt them to a different, natural environment. Everyone here keeps animals. We use horses both for riding and for pulling light carriages. This causes less wear and tear on the roads – just like these vehicles, our 'cars,' which are driven by Zero Point Energy, if you know what that is."

We did of course. This wonderful, free form of energy exists in the entire Universe – apart from Earth.

"But you soon will have Zero Point energy," assured Ranira. "It is avidly being researched there, but also hushed-up. All Earthlings demand proof. We are not like that; we are willing to take shortcuts instead, and have succeeded well by doing so. We shall now leave the Meeting House to look at something else."

The vehicle that had transported us to the Meeting House was not waiting for us outside. In its place stood a carriage, a type of older model of a horse-drawn Landau, but with sleeker lines and a pair of horses attached. Of course they must have horses! Upon closer inspection, their ears were admittedly longer; the mane and tail, too, and fine, long, slender legs. Lydia had already zoomed up to them and flung her arms around the neck of one, petting and cooing at it. However, the horse was only moderately enthralled with all this fuss, and threw its head backwards with a neigh that sounded just like any other horse.

"Watch out, Lydia!" warned Ranira. "Our horses are not used to strangers. I know how much you love animals, but this is going a little too far."

He barely managed to complete this sentence before Lydia received a sharp kick, throwing her over to the other side of the road, where she landed in flowering bush. Ranira and I rushed to her aid and found her limping and sadly bedraggled. This was a memory that undoubtedly would leave her with a new kind of imprint.

However, the journey by horse and carriage went well otherwise. Lydia sulked a bit for a while, but was soon distracted by appreciating all the beauty of the countryside seen from the carriage in passing. It felt strangely as though the horses' hooves weren't touching the ground, but this could hardly have been possible. We stopped at a place overgrown with grass, for the horses to graze. There stood a transparent building, out of which wonderful music poured forth.

"This is our Music Temple," announced Ranira. "We come here whenever we yearn for musical entertainment – which we frequently do. Music cleanses the spirit, makes one joyful, and warms the heart. Do come in!"

We did so. The music that filled the air caused one's legs to involuntarily keep step with the beat, and was nothing like modern music on Earth. These were merry melodies that practically danced and sang by themselves. There was a dance floor for those who wished to dance, with tables and chairs on the periphery for others who just wanted to sit and enjoy the pleasure of the moment. I hauled Lydia up onto the dance floor and we improvised in tune with the music. It was one of the most wonderful, rare moments to savor from our travels throughout the planets. The place was big and airy, made out of some sort of glass so that one could see through it. Outside there were high-growing plants and exquisitely colorful flowers flapping against the panes. It seemed one was both inside and out at the same time.

When we left the Music Temple, we were elated. I sent a few exultant thoughts to the Masters who had commissioned us here. Andromeda was the best of all. The jewel in the crown was the dancing; nothing could exceed such joy. We climbed into the horse-drawn carriage, both of us humming the last tune played.

We had both dearly wished we could have remained in this wonderful place. The music was still just audible, but regrettably we were only visiting, and Ranira yelled that we had to journey on. The horses had stayed standing outside and cast misgiving glances at us strangers as we approached, whinnying impatiently and scraping their hooves. When we looked about us, we noticed other horses and a number of carriages parked around the Music Temple. Some nice little dogs could be seen lying in a few of the carriages, snoozing and waiting patiently for their owners. I decided there and then that I would introduce a Music Temple into our heavenly realms. It would doubtless be greatly appreciated.

We travelled through the breathtakingly beautiful countryside. We started to glimpse water between the trees. Soon we saw more and more water.

"Are there any dragons here, too?" wondered Lydia.

"Here you can see one of our seas," replied Zoa. "And yes, we most surely do have dragon lizards here; great beasts that can fly. They are gentle, just as long as one doesn't deliberately hurt them. They live by themselves, in what are locally called dragon villages, high up in the mountains. Dragons are partial to living in hollows, where there is plenty of food in the vicinity. A wide variety of species of deer may be found up there. Dragons do not, however, hunt for the sake of killing; they do so purely to eat and survive. We are about to go into the mountains to visit the Abode of Wisdom, where the wisest men and women on the planet live, guarded by the dragons."

"I am so very pleased," I responded. "One can never have too much wisdom. Are these the sages who rule Andromeda?"

"I have to give my answer as both 'yes' and 'no' to that question," Ranira ambiguously responded, with an equivocal expression. "In reality, we all govern here! No one is considered better than the next person, and we are many different races, all of whom live peacefully and well together. You shall see."

27. Healing Houses

We had been travelling a while when I suddenly noticed it no longer was light; the sun had ceased to shine and all the colors of the countryside had become muted. Someone came galloping wildly on a horse, pulling up alongside us. Ranira pulled our horses up to a halt, just as we do on Earth, although I didn't catch the words he simultaneously called out to them. The rider was their daughter, Kyra, and sitting in front of her was a child, who turned out to be her little brother. Zoa dashed out from the carriage and took the boy in her arms. He had apparently fallen and hurt himself, so that one of his legs was bleeding profusely. Ranira gave orders to the horses, and they turned about, changing course and taking a smaller path through the woods. The Wisdom visit was going to have to be postponed.

"I heard them mention a hospital," whispered Lydia into my ear. So we will after all see what a hospital here looks like, I thought to myself. The horses trotted on at a brisk pace, and we just about managed to catch sight of what was inside the woods. Admittedly dusk was already falling, but there were whisperings and movements all around. Presumably there were both fairies and other ethereal beings there, for I glimpsed some little people running here and there across the pathways, avoiding the fast-moving horses. I saw billowing veils, softly fanning amongst the trees and light entities, hovering back and forth.

"The forest people tend to be a little anxious whenever we hurtle through at such a hurried pace," explained Ranira. "They are quite used to people, but not when rushing around like this. Commotion is abnormal to them, but just now it's an unavoidable necessity. Our little boy's leg is in great pain; he's fainted and must be swiftly treated by a healer. We are almost there now."

There wasn't a single house in sight. The horses stopped by a moss-covered hill, panting and snorting. We were just beyond the very edge of the wood and could see three towering, moss-covered hills that rose up out of the grassy, flower-speckled ground. There were great patches of moss over the entire area, and some tables and chairs set out, just like a café. Zoa jumped out of the carriage, holding the little lad closely in her arms, and I then noticed that there were doors into each hill. She swiftly vanished through one such door, which also happened to be completely moss-clad. Ranira beckoned to us to follow, so we scurried off in the same direction. We stood absolutely still with amazement. There was little doubt that we were inside a hospital! There were beds positioned throughout the whole of the faintly earth-smelling room, and people wearing green clothing were moving everywhere. Most likely doctors and nurses, I thought. Ranira was already sitting at the side of a bed that her child was lying on, while several of the green-clad people encircled the little patient.

"He'll soon be well," said Ranira. "Instant cures are performed here, so we'll be able to take him with us in just a little while. So now you've seen one of our hospitals, although we call them Healing Houses."

He quickly bowed his head over his wife, who was just lifting the boy down from the bed. The dear little mite was still sleeping. I saw no bandages or dressings on his leg; it looked perfectly normal. Zoa appeared to be thanking the ones in green clothing, and immediately beckoned to us to follow her out. Ranira remained inside briefly. We both felt puzzled and perturbed when we once more climbed up into the carriage. Just a couple of minutes later, Ranira jumped up into his driving seat. The horses bolted off back the same way we had come.

"You were not permitted to see how the healing was performed," explained Ranira while the splendid animals happily trotted along the thoroughly kempt road again. "We therefore sealed your eyes for a couple of minutes, so I understand if this caused you to feel a bit strange. The normal procedure when sudden accidents occur is that they are extremely quickly dealt with and healed – you will see no wounds or scars on our son's leg now. These Healing Houses can be found in various places all over the planet. They are often housed inside mounds of soil, for it is most beneficial to be close to Mother Earth when there has been an accident; earth has healing power – but I don't think this has yet been discovered down on planet Earth!"

I refrained from correcting him; it seemed to be generally thought that we were human beings of flesh and blood – we did after all look as though we were – so I just nodded. We had then come back out onto the bigger road and continued onwards in the direction we had originally been heading, but only briefly, for we shortly took a left turn, onto another narrower path. We were ascending – not steeply, but a steady incline. We momentarily stopped while Ranira strapped us in tightly with safety belts, holding us fast both vertically and horizontally. I comprehended that we must be on our way up to the Abode of Wisdom. I have met so many exceedingly wise people in my time that I couldn't help wondering if these eminently wise folk we soon would have the pleasure of meeting really could be any wiser than all the others. After all, everything eventually culminates in Love, in unity, in belief of the One God's power. What more could there be?

I was soon to find out.

The landscape altered dramatically. The soft, lush beauty was gone and was replaced by gray craggy rocks with narrow passages leading through and around them. The scene was reminiscent of the steep southern European roads that spiral upwards in the high mountains. I must confess to finding this journey more than a little daunting, and I advised Lydia not to look down at the very steepest points. It became obvious why the horses had been chosen to convey us there, since they evidently were used to this stark landscape. They trotted along steadily and assuredly, keeping tightly near the cliff face, and despite the fairly sharp incline of the slope, the ground seemed quite smooth and even. The sun had gone to rest and a damp fog enveloped us. Just as abruptly as we had been shaken by the winding steepness, all around us changed yet again.

We found ourselves going along a straight, light road. The formerly lost, lush, green vegetation once again reappeared in all its colorful glory before our disbelieving eyes. We were pretty high up on the mountain and everything there looked completely different. Curtains of green trees with splendidly cascading leaves stroked us as we passed so closely that we could catch hold of them. The ground emanated delightful aromas and we could hear wondrously magical birdsong. The water glittered in amongst the trees most unusually, considering the great height we were at. Emerald green meadows shortly opened out on either side of our carriage and we completely lost sight of the recent, dismally gray, stark surroundings.

We had arrived and were in awe. The road led through a meticulously tended park, where the plants literally outshone one another, each in their own glory. How could it possibly be like this? I hardly thought this thought before our carriage pulled up in front of a shimmering white, castle-like manor house, reposed in the magnificent countryside at the top of the mountain. I came to think of the Hunza people, whom most others on Earth are quite ignorant of; they dwell high up in the Himalayas. The existence of the Hunza people was unknown on Earth up until the beginning of the twentieth century, equally unknown as Agartha has been up until now. I had always envisioned the Hunza environment rather like this. This race of people live up to about 150 years old and the women continue bearing children until they are 70-80 years of age. I have always been amazed that such a land truly exists on Earth, and there I was, setting foot in a similar place, on another planet.

Only I soon discovered it was far less Earthly than it looked.

28. The Abode of Wisdom

I do not intend attempting to describe this abode, for it is, quite simply, physically impossible to do. I leave it to the imagination of the reader to visualize a picture of unsurpassed beauty. Not only was it deliriously beautiful, but also very delicate, so that we barely dared walk in when the glittering door opened for us. We did, however.

Since Ranira walked in front of us with steady, assertive steps, we just followed closely in his footsteps. Zoa had gently settled her sleeping child on soft pillows inside the carriage and someone, who had apparently come out of the house, arrived to watch over the little lad. Zoa hurried to catch up with us and then linked her arm under Lydia's, presumably to give courage and support. My petrified Angel friend had hidden her face in her hands and hadn't dared look up until Zoa went to her.

I was relieved to find it wasn't nearly as slippery as I first thought when I saw the shiny floors inside, and we ascended a wide staircase as though walking on clouds (which we perhaps also were!). A golden portal above the stairs opened up and inside sat, according to our enlightened friend Ranira, the wisest people of many planets – not just Andromeda.

They were sitting in a semi-circle and the whole place was extremely light, as though illuminated. There were eleven persons: five females and five males, but I was unable to define whether the eleventh one was man or woman because of a blindingly strong aura of surrounding light. Not far in front of them a further semi-circle was formed with soft cushions, which were set out for us. In reverence we bowed deeply, and then sank down into the cushions in front of the eleven Masters.

When we looked up, we could see a starry sky that seemed incredibly close, so that one could almost touch it. Of course, it was just an illusion. Soft music became audible and a lovely aroma spread throughout the room. The Eleven were clothed in long, pastel-colored, glittery cloaks or mantles. Suddenly a tall crystal glass appeared before each of us. Number Eleven, who sat in the middle, between the others, signaled to the other ten to raise their goblets in a toast to us. We respectfully raised our glasses in response, and in the midst of this solemn act, I could not help thinking "Bottoms up!" – that's just how I am; incorrigible! Whenever anything is austerely ceremonious, the silliest of human expressions invariably pop into my head. I glanced at Lydia, knowing she is the same. But, I thought, if this is only an illusion, then I'd not like to remain here, for it all just seems too good to be true. I was sincerely hoping they weren't reading my thoughts just then.

The Masters started to speak. I don't know which of them it was, but it sounded as though a male voice rang loudly and clearly out of nowhere.

"Welcome, brothers and sisters from the Earthly spheres! You are awaited! We know that you come from the Angels, but that you also are representatives for the Earth and therefore we turn to that section of our beloved Milky Way.

"The Earth's greatest-ever challenge since the Creation draws nigh. The Milky Way is pure, far purer than you can imagine. Regrettably, a couple of blots have stained this infinite purity, and they must be cleansed. Evil and darkness may not be allowed to taint our celestial nations, for unfortunately they have a tendency to multiply. Precisely this has occurred on Earth. Consequently, a great metamorphosis must be undergone there. The Earth, where it is currently suspended in Space, has been gravely damaged and must be repaired. Soon neither humans nor animals will be able to continue living on the Earth's surface. The plants, and even the trees, will wither and die. Something must be done!

"You, dear visitors, have observed how things are on several of the countless multitudes of other planets. That which you in your dogged egotism refuse to accept – namely, the existence of other forms of life than your own within the Universe – is nothing other than a complete and utter lie. We have been watching you for millions of years, seeing how your smug, egocentric narcissism and inability to recognize great achievements in small things, besides believing yourselves to be uniquely alone in Space, has finally led you to wrack and ruin. You will not be able to continue your existence there for much longer before being plunged into the abyss … so we would like to give you one last warning!"

"The positive must also be permitted to have their say!" a female voice was then heard to say, and continued. "We know that if evil is to be conquered, innocent victims will be sacrificed in the process, for there are many good people on Earth who think differently and understand that it is high time to rectify matters. These are not trifling matters. The battle between good and evil must have a new face, a new goal. You require help, since you have succeeded in running your once-beautiful planet into the ground. Benevolent powers have rallied around for your assistance and are ready, prepared to intervene with help. But in return you must be willing to learn something new, something you haven't dared accept before, because you haven't wanted to believe.

"Naturally you have prophets; you've had them for hundreds of years. They have made prudent and sensible statements, but possibly not quite believed in themselves fully enough – deep down inside, that is. This is how the nature of things always has been. Prophets step forward, shining radiantly lit – or perhaps discreetly, almost invisibly – their words profoundly affecting many, but not all. Then humdrum life returns to normal, i.e., eat or be eaten, regarding not only the animals. Comforts – shall we cling to these or dare we venture to meet an unknown, perhaps uncomfortable phase?

"The time is come that Sister Earth should become aware that she belongs to the great Cosmic Family. This cannot be achieved by haphazardly chucking out pollution, initially in the countryside, and then out into Space, where it shoots around like tiny germs infecting all that is left unguarded. Grave ills will surely follow if these are allowed to run amok. Primarily it is those instilled with the power of money, coupled with an unhealthy lust for glory and fame. Then there are those riddled with avarice, jealousy, and a begrudging nature towards the susceptible, poor, and defenseless. Furthermore, unscrupulous thieves and charlatans are intent upon deceiving decent, conscientious people."

"And to whom do we refer?" came the rhetorical question, voiced by another of the Eleven. "Who are the spearheads, continually crusading for more? Whose vile thoughts urgently require thorough cleansing? Verily I say: It is those holding elevated positions of power.

"The lust for power, by those who have it, rubs off onto others who crave it. Their steely voices coerce others, both the tough and the meek. The latter are always easy prey and end up being overpowered. How many are they who mindlessly follow the flow, lazily daring not to speak up and brace against the current? Far simpler to just go along, evading any danger. Just watch television! So much easier to comfortably sit back and totally avoid thinking for oneself, leaving it to other kindly people to do all the thinking instead.

"No! Something must be done – and will be done, soon. There has been no shortage of warnings, and that which we speak of now has been happening since the existence of man on Earth. They have sown seed on both stony ground and fertile soil. Their interpretation of the Bible's account of how they came into existence is incorrect. There is a great deal that cannot be relied upon in your annals of history. If you had been aware of us, we could have rectified things. But throughout the entire inner space we have been strictly forbidden to interfere with mankind on Earth's own development. Consequently this is how it has turned out."

"A massive transition is now essential," pronounced a new voice of one of the eleven. "Mankind on Earth must be confronted with our very real existence as living, working, and loving individuals, outwardly created in their own image, but inwardly vastly different. We wish to play an active part in this enormous change, helping as much as we can, for we do not believe that human beings are, left to their own devices, capable of carrying out such an altered way of life. It cannot be emphasized too strongly that something of impact must occur, something monumental and tumultuous."

Cries of exultant rejoicing were heard in response. They reverberated throughout the entire chamber, like a burst of joyful mirth, a warm breeze of humanity, with a hint of fragrant roses mixed with violets and vanilla. The thought suddenly jumped into my mind that it somehow felt like "Home," momentarily enfolded into the benevolent humans' everyday world.

All around I could sense Love of the purest, blissful kind – the Love shared by parents and children, between dear friends, the young and old alike. Love that mutates into a song of laughter and jest, dancing, and hope. There are so many good, harmonious, pleasant feelings! Why do we not permit them to pervade our everyday selves? We should praise the everyday things all the more, for that is where we actually dwell. Above all, we ought to strive to make our everyday life fun to awaken to, worthwhile, playful with our imagination, causing laughter within and without ourselves.

The cheers and murmurs were silenced by yet another voice making an announcement. This time it was a woman's. "Listen; I beg your attention, dear friends! We have visitors from Earth! Please, let us not frighten them, but instead make them happy and hopeful. We wish to eradicate an old expression that has been liberally misused on Earth: 'You only live once!'

"This is totally idiotic and incorrect! How is it possible to even think such nonsense? We live several lives in order to gain knowledge and, hopefully, eventually attain a sufficiently high level of development, enabling us to pass over the threshold into eternity. One must live many lives in order to gradually improve one's karma. Animals also live numerous lives and can change dramatically. This is not the case with humans, however, since their change is solely inward, preparing them for becoming one with the light. But they never lose their one identity, which is their soul. The soul has eternal life.

"I doubt I am telling you anything new with this, but it is my belief that if people really and truly accepted the fact that they have the ability to improve their souls, thereby elevating them to a level higher, then the vast majority would be far more vigilant in their words and thoughts. Thought is the instrument for unimaginably pleasurable experiences within the Cosmos. Thought is every individual's very own Pegasus.

Thought is the most important thing of all. Just like us, human beings ought from infancy to learn how to control their thoughts. By doing so, your society would totally alter!"

Indeed this was nothing at all new to us. But it was an important reminder, a prompt that could move mountains. There are so many words, but they don't always imprint themselves as they ought. I glanced at Lydia. She was sitting erect in the lotus position, on the burgundy-colored velvet cushion, with gentle tears running slowly down her cheeks while her lips smiled.

Then again, there are a multitude of different levels. I didn't even attempt to envision all the different levels where the words of the Wisest would be scrumpled up and tossed into the waste-paper basket. It was better to imagine them as little birds, flying into human hearts and settling there to rest. Ranira had been referring to the Wisest in the World. But isn't ordinary wisdom ("common sense") also valid as being the highest aspiration of those seeking? Let us regard ordinary wisdom as a first step up. The next step is not quite as remote as it might seem, high up amongst the clouds – it may in fact be much closer than you imagine. And suddenly it all runs along like clockwork.

It seemed as though the eleven did not have anything more to add, with the exception of the eleventh one (who was so difficult to define the sex of), who moved just in front of the other ten, looked intensely at Lydia and me, and said, "You two eminent spirits who have trodden Mother Earth with your feet, listen to me now! You have visited other planets, and we were not really included in your designated program. Perhaps we are too human-like, although we do not live like humans on Earth. Your rulers ought to pay us a visit in order to learn something useful. Perhaps this might happen, one way or another, since the Earth is going to be altered.

"You must totally change your way of thinking. You have to understand that the entire, infinite Space is full of life, and that life can take many forms. Your films made about extraterrestrials are sometimes surprisingly accurate, apart from all the hostile battling. Naturally, wars have taken place in Space; there are always a few power-seeking buffoons, but so far they have been effectively counter-attacked. What you would describe as magic is to us just a natural part of life. What you consider great inventions are to us simple and straightforward things. What you call governments, we regard as power-madness and abuse of the inner wisdom. So you certainly have much to learn!

"We wish you good luck on your continued journey. We are always here, and should you wish to contact us, you are always welcome to do so directly or via our intermediaries: Helis the Sun man and Hella the Sun woman!"

A gentleman and a lady stepped down from the podium, walked straight over, and embraced us. Helis and Hella! These were our new contacts. They bade us only to think of them whenever we needed their assistance, and they would provide us with answers. We respectfully bowed and backed out of the chamber, together with Ranira. Lydia, of course, characteristically tripped over her long skirt and loudly landed splat on the floor, so that all could hear. I rushed to help her up, simultaneously glancing nervously towards the podium. I was met by many smiles, so there was evidently no lack of humor up there!

29. Visiting the Reptilians

"You've been given much to think about," said Ranira, stating the obvious with a good-humored smile, as we clambered in our little carriage after having patted the horses and given them a few encouraging words. I turned around and gave the beautiful house an appreciative, farewell glance. Lydia's flood of tears was escalating and she soon started sobbing loudly into Zoa's shoulder, so that Ranira had to remove his little boy onto his lap. I understood that the physically embodied Lydia had been deeply moved by all the beauty and gravity that we had just experienced, awakening old memories of her last life on Earth that pained her. But our own recollections of previous lives on Earth were not to interfere with our mission, which I was forced to remind her of. Furthermore, we soon had a great deal else to think about.

Dusk had fallen, just as it would have done at home. Zoa's and Ranira's little son sat in the carriage with an older lady when we arrived. She had a friendly face and was apparently telling him stories, for he was agog, listening intently with mouth wide open. It felt safe and comfortable, with a pleasant horsey smell, so familiar from times on Earth. The horses trotted on at a fairly quick pace, seemingly eager to get beyond the worst part of the road along the cliff face before the blackness of nightfall. I don't know how we managed to come down so quickly, but all of a sudden we found ourselves driving along the straight stretch of road, just as total darkness fell. However, our lanterns had lit up, both inside the carriage and out. There were also lanterns on the horses – even their bridles and reins shone with a bright, clear light. I don't think anything quite like this had yet been invented on Earth!

It didn't take very long to reach Ranira's house. A somewhat irate Kyra came out to meet us; she felt left out and would have liked to accompany us on our meeting with the Wisest. Ranira had to promise her that they soon would visit them again.

"Perhaps it is time that we should prepare to return home again?" I pondered, as we settled down in their comfortable living room (dining room cum study, cum television room, etc. …) and chatted about the day's adventures.

Ranira twisted around uncomfortably. "No," he finally blurted out, "I'm afraid you cannot go back quite yet. I have been given further orders to take you to another planet. You are to visit a reptilian planet. There are many such planets within the Universe, and you should be familiar with them."

"Not I!" screamed Lydia. "Ooh, I really don't want to. Please, not reptiles! I have a dreadful fear of snakes, big lizards, and …"

"Dragons?" I helpfully added.

"Dragons aren't reptiles," snapped Lydia. "Dragons are wonderful, great, lovely, wise, kind … um hmm …"

"Lovely, wise, kind what?" interrupted Ranira, laughing. "Dragons are the archetype for the reptilians. I think it's best that you come along; otherwise you will not have completed your mission. We can hold on to you, if you are frightened."

And so it was. Lydia meekly followed along after having, with Zoa's help, changed into a more suitable outfit á la tropics, i.e., high boots, white suit, and pith helmet, which suited her down to the ground.

We gentlemen put on something similar, and then we all settled ourselves into the "car." No time for relaxation in peace and quiet in these spheres. This time Zoa did not join us, but Kyra did instead. We once again set off on a new expedition. It hardly seemed possible that anything could surpass the incredibly wonderful visit to Andromeda.

The journey in the "car" took us to an extraordinary airfield. It was extraordinary in the sense that although it looked like an Earthly airfield, it was the farthest thing from it. All the craft there were spaceships in various forms – and I really do mean various. Not a single one was at all like any other. It was extremely colorful and rather noisy in the enormous parking area. Apparently, one didn't need to queue up at a ticket window; Ranira just drove straight up to a spaceship and parked the "car" right there, and we were signaled to go aboard. He vanished with his vehicle while we climbed up a fairly strongly built ladder and then sat ourselves down in the rather cramped cabin. Seated inside were already a number of people – or beings?

"We're now taking off for Eta Draconis," informed Ranira, who had suddenly appeared and sat in front of us, next to Kyra. "Eta Draconis is the oldest of draconian and reptilian planets. Your arrival is awaited, and you will be extremely well met. They used to be warlike, but as recently as the 1990s everything changed for them. You will learn more after we arrive there."

Behind us sat a couple, presumably draconians. Their heads were conspicuously dragon-like, their eyes yellowish, and mouths extremely large and wide. They had no hair and their skin was bright green and scaly. They tried to be friendly and smiled at us, which contorted their faces into the most hideous masks. I smiled back at them and they then settled down, seemingly satisfied with the humans' conduct. Inwardly I was cowering at the thought of having to meet a mass of similarly bizarre individuals. The only consolation was that we, presumably in their eyes, were equally peculiar. Lydia had fallen asleep; it had been an exhausting day.

The journey to the Dragon Planet went quickly. In fact, it only seemed as though a couple of minutes had passed when Ranira shook my shoulder.

"Don't sleep; we're just about to land!" he shouted into my ear. There were the most dreadful crashing and banging sounds as we hit the ground, and the spaceship wobbled back and forth until it finally came to a complete halt. I remained in my seat until the dragon-headed ones had rushed out of the vessel. Then I awakened Lydia. At the bottom of the ladder Ranira and his daughter stood waiting for us.

Behind them I could see a mass of dragon and lizard-headed beings, dressed in ordinary clothes, enthusiastically waving at us, as though we were Royalty. As usual, Lydia immediately made the most of the situation and graciously smiled and waved back. I caught on that it was her intention to play the regal role of Queen until she clearly could see what we had landed ourselves in.

I went over to Ranira and a peculiar man with a crocodile head, wearing a uniform, who came to meet us. A great roar of laughter suddenly broke out amongst the people behind him, and I turned around in surprise. All I could see was Lydia's enchanting backside and a furious woman picking herself up off the ground. She had evidently tripped on the steps when showing off, proudly holding her head too far back to see where she put her feet. So there she landed too ungainly on the ground, a source of great amusement to the crowd. Some of the lizard people rushed forward to assist her, which Lydia did not appreciate. She attempted to hold herself perfectly upright and, with an unperturbed expression, strode over to me, more or less oblivious of her rather strange new environment. The laughter had ceased, but the kindly concern for Lydia's wellbeing remained, indicating to me that these were special people.

"They apologize for not having at once warned your companion about how slippery it is here," said Ranira quietly to me. I repeatedly smiled and nodded while whispering to Lydia to do likewise. She instantly altered her haughty expression to one of benevolent gratitude, shaking hands with all who flocked around her.

Kyra, who had watched the whole incident with unconcealed delight, shouted to anyone willing to hear, "This is just our usual manner of greeting whenever we visit a new planet!" In this way, Lydia was saved from feeling embarrassed and bewildered.

The man in the uniform whom Ranira was speaking to seemed to be very high ranking. A small lizard woman, who had managed to sneak in between Lydia and Kyra, bellowed out in a loud voice, "We have sent Pyriocanin, who is in command here, to meet you. He will escort you to the Palace, where you are to be presented to our Royal Highnesses and dine with them." She subsequently bowed deeply to us and then vanished.

The man in the white uniform, looking as though he'd almost lost his concentration, loudly cleared his throat and announced, "You are most welcome here, and it is my great pleasure to escort you to our Regents, who have so impatiently awaited your arrival ever since they heard you were on your way here."

He bowed, causing all the golden bands, epaulettes, and chains on his uniform to jingle merrily. Then he led us down to two vehicles that looked even more extraordinary than usual. Gigantic lizards, or more likely dragons, stepped forward and bent down right in front of us. On second thought, I realized they probably were a variety of lizard, since their heads were considerably smaller than a dragon's and mostly resembled a turtle's, with an elongated nose.

We didn't dare hesitate. Ranira went straight up and mounted the first one, closely followed by Kyra, leaving the second one free for Lydia and me to seat ourselves upon. The great beasts were fitted with the most elegant, gold-embellished saddles that were surprisingly comfortable to sit in. It understandably felt a little shaky as they stood up to their full height, and worse still, when they spread out their wings and took flight. We had involuntarily become dragon-riders, whether we liked it or not. But we were actually sitting pretty securely inside a golden cage, close to one another and tightly secured with glistening straps. Naturally, Lydia was absolutely petrified, but there was some comfort for both of us that we were sitting together supportively. I dare say Kyra felt the same.

I giggled at the thought that camel rides here would be dragon rides instead!

The landscape below held no great surprise to us. All the planets are comprised of mountains, hills, lakes, sea, forests, deserts, and agricultural land. Here, too – only the proportions were somewhat greater than we'd seen before. When the palace came into view below, it was of course gigantic. Our "live airplane" descended gradually and carefully, until landing in the valley, where the palace lay like a jewel embedded in the luscious greenery.

I finally concluded that it was after all a dragon's head I patted, once I had set my feet down on terra firma again – only somehow smaller and kinder. Lydia had turned all limp and pale when Kyra came rushing over to us with eyes lit up, excitedly yelling, "Ooh that was soooo fantastic! We just have to introduce this type of transport to our planet, too! I shall beg Daddy to ask …"

She disappeared back over to her father as quickly as she had arrived. Ranira was walking with the General, or whatever his title was, and we joined them.

We had apparently landed directly outside the palace, for an enormous door opened before us, and we stepped in. Then another gigantic door opened up for us and, after that, yet a third one – all were equally huge.

"This is not an area where vehicles are permitted to enter," announced the General. "This in itself ensures the safety of the palace; furthermore, there's a deep, surrounding moat that the dragons flew you across. We're about to enter the lobby."

After passing through the lobby, there were a further two lobbies – enormous of course – decorated with fittingly large-scale statues and other art. Then, at long last, we finally reached the Royal Couple's reception room.

It wasn't dreadfully huge, but just about as homely as a dragon's room can be. It was full of statues and paintings, but also afforded comfortable seating of various proportions, and tables with cloths of gold brocade. The Royal Couple were something out of this world – or perhaps I should say, the reptilian world! We did not find them, as is customary, sitting on exalted thrones. Quite the contrary, for they were lying on the floor, absorbedly playing games with their little children (not denoting the latter's size, but presumed tender age).

The Queen was the first to arise, brushing off her brocade as she moved towards us. I wonder if you ever, perchance, have embraced a crocodile? If not, I would strongly advise you to forego this dubious pleasure! Both Lydia and I were still coughing violently for quite some time afterwards. Then it was the King's turn! Luckily for us, he greeted us a little more carefully, by patting only us gentlemen on the shoulders – causing our knees to give way underneath us – and amicably squeezing our hands. We never felt the handshake, for our entire hands vanished inside his claws.

"Thank you for coming here!" he growled and then whinnied, which presumably was his form of laughter. Lydia put an arm around Kyra, who at last was showing signs of feeling a little afraid.

"Let us then dine!" proclaimed the Queen. "Then we may converse with our celebrated guests. I am longing to hear all you have to tell about Earth and the other planets you have visited. We have much to discuss, my dears!"

With mixed feelings, I meekly followed along with the others to the dining room (or should I say banquet hall?), it, too, being gigantic, of course. A smaller table was laid in one corner of the room, at which we sat. I inwardly shuddered at the thought of what we might politely have to eat.

We enjoyed a lively conversation, with no pregnant pauses, recounting our planetary journeys to the best of our ability. The food, however, turned out to be a great surprise. We were served a most delicious variety of vegetarian dishes. The King and Queen ate something different, in far greater portions – but I had no wish to know what it was. Actually I was just happy that it had turned out to be such a superbly splendid and most amiable meal. Afterwards, we went out into the exceedingly beautiful and well looked after garden – but enormous, too, of course. Our Royal hosts truly made a great effort to be hospitable and entertaining, totally succeeding in dispelling any fears we may have had – to the point of all four of us forgetting that we were in the company of elevated Royalty (in the best possible way).

Having enjoyed a genuinely lovely spell in the garden, it was time for a little sight-seeing. The massive modes of transport, with their huge lizard heads – or small crocodile ones, whatever it was they were – immediately came flying over and parked themselves as near to us as they conceivably were able. The General, with the strangest imaginable name, had been with us the whole time and was also to be our guide on our tour. The King and Queen returned to their duties, as they called them, and waved us off after we'd settled ourselves into the saddle-cages.

We waved back in a final farewell to our regal visit – or so we thought.

"What a relief not to have to stand in ceremony any longer!" yelled Lydia, as the powerful wings lifted us off the ground with a loud bang. "One has such a splendid view from up here, and you know, Janne, I can talk to these two Pegasuses, but one has to be very close to their ears. I've named them Happy and Doc, like in the tale of Snow White and the Seven Dwarfs."

"Pegasus was a winged horse," I interjected, "born out of the fountain of blood that spurted out when Medusa was beheaded by Perseus."

Lydia laughed, being a historian. "Oh, those ancient myths!" she retorted. "Can't one journey within them in the same way we travel amongst the planets? I love stories, and I would really like to go on an expedition in them. Why, we could ask the Pilgrim when we see him again!" But I had ceased listening to her.

"Look, what a strange sort of landscape!" I shouted.

Lydia leaned over sideways, simultaneously gripping my arm tightly. Down below must have been some sort of jungle; not the usual, verdant, inviting jungle, but a brushwood – a leafless jungle of stark, knotted, entwined branches with brown water in between, that looked like a swamp. It looked undeniably singular and impassable, which made me sincerely hope we weren't going to go down into it, since our transport was lowered itself and nearing the treetops. The murky water we occasionally caught a glimpse of looked anything other than inviting. Our transport weaved its way onwards and, in doing so, broke a few parched twigs that cracked loudly, but we did not land, thank heavens!

All of a sudden we were flying alongside the others, and the General, who was sitting on the neck of the other dragon-lizard, called out, "We won't be landing here; there are swamp folk down there. There are many such swamps in various places. The swamp folk there are partial to stealing – both people and belongings. We cannot allow this sort of thing. Sometimes they do battle with us, but we usually win." He gave out a startling laugh that sounded more like croaking.

With my inner eye I could see how ghastly such a war must be and prayed that we soon would reach a more pleasant area. I didn't have to wait long. The twisted swamplands soon gave way to beautifully verdant meadows. It was on one of these that we eventually descended and started to graze. No, not we people, of course, but our "vehicles" apparently were herbivores and needed re-fuelling. The General instantly ran over to us. His crocodile face radiated benevolence and his large mouth smiled widely. I would have preferred not to see exactly how many teeth he had, long and sharp as they were.

Wherever we came to on other planets, feasting seemed to be simple and efficiently procured. So also in this beautiful meadow, for there, on a perfectly ordinary tree stump, a tray of delectable drinks and appetizingly sweetened bread had been placed for us. Evidently a great deal of honey was used in cooking, so I inquired to ascertain if this was so.

"Indeed, we use honey in almost all our food," replied the General. "The bees are our best friends, and we see to it that they are well looked after. There are beehives all over the place, in towns and in the country – even up in certain trees. How lovely to hear you also appreciate honey! We will now fly over another swamp area. When we have passed it you will see one of our towns."

I noticed that Kyra was both touched and exhausted, so I was beginning to wonder if it was a wise decision to bring her with us. I gave her an encouraging smile.

"I have to say," continued the General, "that our dear animals of flight are exceedingly partial to a particular plant that grows solely in the swamplands. Please do not be alarmed if they stop at the next swamp to eat, but I must ask that you remain in your saddle-cages. Under no circumstances are you to remove yourselves from your saddled positions, whatever you may see. I will ensure that they very swiftly take off into the air again, should they fleetingly wish to land there to eat. They are usually most reasonable creatures, our flying 'taxis.'"

We journeyed on. I began to feel a little sleepy and observed Lydia's eyelids drooping, too. Truth to say, it was a bit monotonous, flying around in this manner, even if it did feel safe. I fell asleep. I was rudely awakened from my slumbers by a loud bang and was terrified to see that our beast thudded to the ground next to its mate. Both of them lost no time in grazing as fast as they could manage.

"Remain in your seats!" bellowed the General and Ranira in unison. Lydia had also woken up and we looked around us. That which was not to happen had happened.

30. Dangerous Swamplands

It smelled peculiar. We found ourselves in the midst of the swampland and the light was fading. Happy and Doc alternately lay, sat, and moved slowly across an overgrown meadow. Tall, bare trees surrounded the great mass of vegetation, apparently so irresistibly yummy to our flying friends. They gulped it down so greedily that one could hear nothing other than their loud munching, for it sounded like a dozen airplanes buzzing in the air.

However, this was not the only thing happening. Very slowly, people (if that's what they were?) were stealthily closing in on us. Once again, it's not easy to describe these "people," because they all had human bodies, but crowned with an astonishing variety of heads. They were completely naked, although the majority were thickly covered in hair. The initial impression I received was that they looked rather more like animals walking upright on their hind legs. However, this first impression soon changed, once I'd noticed how precise and smooth their completely human movements were, besides the way they carried their arrows over their shoulders. They did not look particularly amiable. Their eyes, or at least as much of their eyes as one could glimpse through all the straggly tufts of hair, had a look of coldness and cruelty about them.

The General then yelled out, "Try to coerce your transport agents to take flight now!"

Kyra had whispered into our beast's ear, "Please do likewise!"

It turned out to be Lydia, of course, who finally came upon the brilliant idea to whisper a promise of lots of delectable food awaiting them elsewhere, and anything else that sprang into her keen imagination, provided we moved on quickly. One of the opposition's strange beasts had made its way right up to our lizard-dragon when our co-pilot's one slowly took off with its mouth stuffed full. In order to speak into our beast's ear, Lydia had to momentarily hang onto its neck. At that very moment, one of the archers managed to grab hold of one of her feet, so I jumped out of our cage to pull her back. Presumably, our beast had at last appreciated the impending danger, and in the nick of time, notwithstanding a final mouthful of plants, took flight, leaving behind the belligerent men below with only the shoe, so that Lydia, otherwise unscathed, then was safely held in my arms. I heaved us into the cage and safely secured us into our saddles, closing the gate tightly. Our most blessed primeval beast intrepidly soared up into the sky while Lydia pressed herself against me and, as usual, sobbed away.

"This is a nasty, horrible planet, and I don't want to stay here," she sniffed. "I adore Happy and Doc, but I can't take all this much longer. I want to go home, pleeeease!"

In the meantime, we remained safely in our cage until the next landing. This was in the middle of what they called "town," which didn't much correspond with my idea of the word. Certainly there were bigger, higher buildings standing closer together. These were in a variety of shapes and made out of some gray material. Some had transparent green domes; others had unique projections, extending one house into two.

The General jumped down to the ground and beckoned to us to follow suit. Lydia had applied her ability to create a new pair of comfortable white shoes with sensible heels. She had by that time furthermore recovered from the preceding traumatic incident, merrily patted our beats of flight on their noses, and skipped off, in pursuit of our guide in the cobble-stoned square that resembled the Old Town back home in Stockholm. The whole place had a dingy, gray look about it, but when the General proudly made a sweeping gesture with his hands towards all around us and asked if we thought it pleasing to the eye, we politely nodded without enthusiasm.

Folk were milling around as far as the eye could see, and it was not difficult to guess that they must live in the area. Their heads and upper parts of their bodies looked like a variety of animals, mostly crocodiles or lizards, but there were some indescribable, assorted mixtures, too.

The lower parts of their bodies appeared to have ordinary human legs that they walked, ran, or jumped about with, just as we do. There were a great many of them, shoving and pushing their way through the crowds, shouting, yelling, and brazenly staring at us. The General made sure they didn't get too close to us, by appointing a ring of big, strong people between ourselves and the indiscernible mass. We entered a tall, circular building that was as gray inside as out and smelled strongly of damp and mold.

"This is our Community Center," declared the enthusiastic General. "This is where we hold performances, exhibitions (of what, he didn't say), council, and other meetings. Isn't it perfectly wonderful here?" We nodded and smiled benevolently the whole time; it was the only thing we could do.

Obviously, not all inhabited planets can be populated with solely humans. We humans are far too egocentric for our own good. This is a bad attitude that we really must learn to change – and perhaps sooner than we imagine – when the worlds meet in cosmic fraternity. We shall have to learn to accept and respect one another. This I knew, but apparently not our frightened, little, unpredictable Lydia. A more cowardly Angel would be hard to find! She crouched behind my back and seemed to have gone completely dotty.

Inside, the building reminded me of my old school – not a particularly pleasant memory. Everything was gray, and a gray stone staircase led up to the floor above, where all again was equally gray. The General was ecstatic, and I was finding it hard to keep up with his fervent capriciousness. I soon began to feel as gray as everything else around me, so that I felt a sense of great relief when the General suggested we break for dinner. I then planned to propose we excuse ourselves, on the premise of having to return to our home planet by a certain time.

It seemed as though there was an awareness of time on this planet. It would have been pointless to say that we weren't actually travelling to any planet at all, since no one there would have understood what we meant. The people there evidently believed that the whole of Outer

185

Space was exactly the same as where they lived, and considered us to be some sort of supernatural being – judging by the General's knowing nods, winks, and contortions of his face. His crocodile teeth sparkled against his greenish-brown face.

"It's pretty calm in our country just at present," explained the General. "We are frequently at war here otherwise. Our king is a weak character and certainly no strategist, so we're hoping to be rid of him soon. When that happens, it won't be a lot of fun to be here, watching the uprising storm loom. I am aware that something unavoidably great is about to take place on Earth, causing you to have more than your fair share of cleansing. Please, would you be so kind as to spare us a positive thought now and then?"

This I faithfully promised. Lydia had caught sight of something that looked like a zoological garden amidst all the gray houses. The General invited us for an afternoon in the gardens, which made Lydia feel satisfied. All her fear and exhaustion simply vanished.

"Do we have the same God?" I asked the General, who responded by smiling with delight. Lydia and the others had gone off on foot on their own little safari around the high fences.

"Visitors are in no danger here," he assured me. "In answer to your question, I would like to say yes, one could say that we do. On this entire planet we all worship only one God of creation – those wild types who took Lydia's shoe included." He whinnied like a horse and – for a split second – I thought he actually looked like one. "There is an unwritten law that we worship God, but recently an awful lot of sub-gods seem to have popped up. They do not have anywhere near the power of our Father Almighty ruling God, but they have been adapted to suit many different tribes here. Do you know what I mean?"

I nodded and decided to leave it at that. One could perhaps say that all our various religions correspond to their sub-gods.

By the time Lydia, Kyra, and Ranira returned, the General and I had exhausted all the questions concerning the planet's committees and various social laws. It was noteworthy that the reptilian planet turned out to be one of the few planets and stars we had visited that wasn't perfect. But despite this, it was a far cry from how it was on Earth, and most unlikely that it could influence us in any way.

The methods of governing and fundamental values on most of the planets we visited were pretty much alike. The basis of all these societies is Love, a Love which is based on a genuine, inner compassion for the development of the soul and a genuine, outward reaching compassion for each other. Upon this basis rest four Divine Laws, inspired by the Spiritual Hierarchy. These Four Basic Societal Laws are as follows:

Law of the One: The goal of every being is to discover their soul path for personal growth and service.

Law of the Two: The power of Creation is experienced in a loving relationship with another being. This closeness defines the couple's divine service to each other and to others.

Law of the Three: The close bond with one's self, friends, family, and clan creates the planetary web. Within the planetary web, we rely on each other's strength to create a greater strength.

Law of the Four: The Law of the Four is the Law of the Three expanded to larger groups, such as clan-to-clan and planetary-to-star-nation.

In order to help one another apply these Love-motivated Laws, a Galactic Society is often organized into what one can call Podlets. A podlet is composed of up to sixty-four people following similar paths in life – for example: healers, spiritual ancestors, engineers, scientists, etc. Within the podlet the older ones give educational support and guidance to the younger ones. Knowledge and wisdom is valued very highly. The pedagogical aim is to build up a high degree of self-esteem and personal independence, besides maximizing Joy and Love within every individual.

The greater "grouping" that encloses and supports a podlet is called a Pod, which encompasses up to 500 podlets. On the next level is the Clan, which comprises up to 11,000 pods. Further to this, a greater number of Clans form a Star Nation. An important basic principle is that the individual is given support, sustenance, and strength by society, so that the individual may contribute their strength to society in return.

This is roughly how I would describe the governing methods within our Space. I pondered this point while sitting in my comfortable seat, flying back to Andromeda, where Kyra and her father lived.

During our travels throughout the various planets, we have met Kings and Queens – and marveled! On Earth they soon will become extinct; no countries have Kings and Queens who truly reign any longer. Monarchs nowadays are simply decorative figureheads, as on the prow of a ship. No one asks their advice, for they cannot answer freely; only the wind may speak to them – and the wind is too bright and breezy to care. The Earth's monarchs are in name only, merely posing as regents. On other planets they hold an esteemed position and importantly participate in everything. They take command of the ship and, for the most part, succeed in steering it through the raging seas and riding out the storm.

At the same time, the people actively participate within their allotted groups, in which they apply their unlimited power and knowledge. If an error is made somewhere, then everyone pulls together to help. We have so much to learn from our neighbors out in Space, for nowhere is freedom confined, other than on Earth. What really is happening is that we are on the brink of a liberation that is so overwhelmingly enormous and genuine that it is making Space history!

"Your forehead is as wrinkly as a walnut!" Lydia's gleeful voice rang out. We had reached the field where our spaceship stood ready to take us to … well, exactly where, we didn't yet know, but most likely back to Earth. The General had accompanied us the whole way, enthusiastically chatting to Ranira while I was deep in thought. Kyra skipped about, this way and that, curious about everything. Every now and then she interrupted her father's conversation with the General. The strange thing was that the planet we were about to leave was the very one most reminiscent of Earth, at least regarding its negative structure. Its countryside also had much in common with ours, but possibly slightly more stark.

All of a sudden it felt strangely odd to be leaving just then, but Lydia was determined. I don't believe Kyra was too keen on the idea of staying there any longer either; she was becoming homesick.

"Well, how do you feel now?" inquired Ranira, once we had politely taken our leave and settled ourselves into the spaceship. I recounted a few of my thoughts and told him I was a bit relieved to end this visit. At the same time, I couldn't help pondering why people are so afraid of all that is new and different from us — terrified of all that deviates from how we see ourselves and conceive the world. But of course by then I had already been given the answer. Wouldn't you agree, my dear sisters and brothers on Earth: Everything should be just the same as we think, are used to, and like it to be? The very thought of strange human bodies with animal heads moving amongst us is quite unbearable. We simply cannot tolerate anomalies, isn't it so?

So, what then is Love, if we are unable to accept All?

31. Amelioration or Decline

This was the question I put to the Pilgrim, since he happened to be the first person we saw as we walked down the gangplank. We had landed outside Ranira and Kyra's home on the beautiful Andromedan planet. We hadn't needed to call for help, yet precisely that was what I held in my thoughts, and quite possibly the others did, too: a simple cry for help. I desired Love, but was never certain if what I felt was adequate.

Lydia and Lissa tumbled around in the grass, while I put the question to the Pilgrim, for I no longer had the strength to bear it any longer. How does one get Love to be sufficient and to be lasting?

"The only way is to transform yourself, both your inner and outer self, to Love," the Pilgrim responded with a warm smile. "I thought you knew this, Jan, my dear friend! If one wishes to be Love, one must radiate Love and think Love. To be Love, all the way through, is one of the most difficult things of all."

"You are," I mumbled, and added, "Even though I still don't know who you are …"

"Before you travel back to your Heavenly dwelling, you shall know!" he promised, smiling.

Zoa came out of the house and invited us to go in and have supper. I searched for the Sun; presumably it was just setting, for I no longer could see it. Lydia danced in ahead of me, absolutely beside herself in joyful anticipation of our homeward journey. But this was not to be quite as soon as she thought.

"I have something to tell you," announced Zoa, as soon as we had concluded our superb, vegetarian supper. Still being in our physical bodies, we had especially enjoyed the delicious food. "While you were on the reptilian planet, apparently having the most wonderful time," she said with a touch of ire, "I was contacted by the Three Games."

"Pains!" exclaimed Lydia, alarmed, "Good gracious – did they hurt terribly?" Kyra could not hold back a fit of loud giggles and shot out of the room.

"Not pains, dear Lydia! – Games, but I thank you for your concern," smiled Zoa.

"The Games are a sort of communication system we have here," interjected the Pilgrim by way of explanation. "Sometimes we find it better with a living message than those written on the wall."

"Quite so," continued Zoa. "We were scolded for not having informed them that you were here visiting. This ought to have been one of our top priorities and it was most remiss of us. Naturally, I apologized profusely. But I was also made to promise that upon your return you would meet some of our governors to exchange information. You will of course stay overnight in our guest rooms. They will come here to collect you early tomorrow morning."

"Oh, and I thought we would be returning home now!" croaked Lydia, somewhat dismayed.

"And so you shall, very soon!" the Pilgrim nodded assent. "Only this time, Lissa and I will be accompanying you, if you feel that might be of help!"

It most certainly did. And so it came about that we spent the night in their most comfortable, singular house, and sleep rejuvenated us, giving strength to face yet another mysterious day.

The mysterious and unforeseen day radiated warmth and shone upon us when we awakened to the ringing of the breakfast bell. The bathroom, equipped very much like those on Earth, was visited with a great deal of hustle and bustle, and a bright-eyed, rosy-faced Lydia emerged in a pale blue, pearl-embroidered trouser suit. We barely managed to finish our breakfast when a hovercraft stood ready for us outside the door, which we made haste to climb into. There, grinning away, sat the Pilgrim with Lissa. I observed that whenever Lissa was around, Lydia hadn't a worry in the world. Apparently, neither did the Pilgrim have any idea where we were to be taken – or he wouldn't say. Then, all of a sudden, we sailed off into a blue mist.

Was it into Space, or to a new planet we were on our way to? The Pilgrim, who was seated in front of us, turned around, beaming from ear to ear. "Now I know where we're going!" he revealed. "We are on our dear Earth, only a bit underneath!"

"I know!" shrieked Lydia triumphantly, "We are in the capital of Agartha: Shamballa."

"There were some there who wished to meet you," continued the Pilgrim. "They have a very important message for you to take with you to the Heavenly Spheres. It's apparently something you are to carry in your luggage."

Agartha's shimmering, mother-of-pearl buildings have unsurpassable beauty and elegance. Some are rather imposing, but not in a ghastly way, just extremely lavish. It is a learning center that contains absolutely EVERYTHING, but only in the best possible sense.

We absorbed everything our hungry eyes fell upon. We no longer were in our physical, human form, for mostly five-dimensional beings were to be seen in Shamballa. What about dogs? When we looked at Lissa, she held herself in a new, proud manner, with nose pointing forward and tail raised high. She gleamed all over; the whole dog shimmered from head to tail, which made me wonder whether we also shimmered. I never needed to ask, because when I glanced at Lydia, she closely resembled a sparkler lit at Christmas. Presumably I did, too, but I didn't want to know. I just wanted to know why it was so urgent that we visit this fantastically splendid city.

The glimmering Pilgrim walked in front of us, straight through a door. My eyes were actually starting to smart from all the sparks around me; the light was so incredibly bright. As usual, we followed closely in his footsteps. I have never seen a dog carry herself as Lissa did. She walked as though she were a Queen, with head constantly held high and mostly her tail, too. I can well understand why my Angel friend was so fascinated by her.

Oddly enough, I almost started to wish that everything hadn't been quite so perfect and flawless. A feeling of monotonous boredom struck me.

The Pilgrim had been observing me, somewhat amusedly. "It's a common reaction, Janne," he commented, encouragingly. "It's just too good to be true. The human being is a most complex individual. But take a better look around you now!"

We had arrived at a rather large room. It wasn't nearly as ostentatiously elegant as the way leading to it had been; in fact, it was quite ordinary and extremely pleasant. A great open fireplace threw out its wonderful warmth. When I stopped to reflect, the way to this room had actually been rather chilly. A circle of comfortable chairs was placed in front of the fire; I counted seven of them. The Pilgrim invited us to sit down, so we each nestled comfortably into an armchair on either side of him. The other chairs were unoccupied.

At first there was complete silence. Then I smelled an aromatic waft of juniper from the fire, and soft music sounded. Four people in glittering gold cloaks entered, bowed to us, and sat down in the empty armchairs. They were none other than Master Saint Germain, Master Melchizedek, Master El Morya, and the female Master, Lady Nada. But I missed Master Lanto; he was seldom very far from Saint Germain. At that point the Pilgrim arose, threw off his pilgrim's habit, and stood there in exactly the same type of glittering gold cloak as the others wore. He bowed to us.

"My dear friends," he said, looking at us with mirth in his eyes, "please permit me to introduce myself: My name is Lanto!"

The solemnity of the atmosphere was dispelled by a bark from Lissa. Everyone started to laugh, and there were joy and hugs all around. I felt totally elated. This surely was a most wonderful ending to our planetary journeys. I knew each and every one of these Masters, and loved them like brothers. And for Lydia, Lady Nada was a sister. In some way we already had come home.

Saint Germain started to speak, "We just wanted to proffer a few words of farewell to you from Earthly Agartha, for you to take with you on your journey and remember up there in your Heavenly realms. In truth, this is not so much for the benefit of you two, Lydia and Jan, as for my readers of this book. There are veritably stormy times coming shortly to our beautiful Earth, and the people need to be prepared for all the tumult.

"As you most certainly know, even though you no longer live on the surface of the Earth, the wicked age of crime, hatred, jealousy, and lust for power has rooted itself deeply, so that the Earth is brimming over with the sad consequences. And so it was regrettably intended. Unbeknown to you, the despotic tyrants, Anunnaki, have been ruling you all the time up until now. All the governments on Earth have been dancing to their pipe; they have been faithful and obedient servants of evil personified. However, there are always some good factions, acting according to their own ability, who are not on the forefront, but all the more effective in their lowly positions. In the end – but it has taken this long a time – the Anunnaki must withdraw, since the Earth's multitude of allies throughout the Universe have stood up to bring out the necessary, enormous changes.

"The Earth desperately requires help, and help is on its way – the wheels have already been set in motion! By the time Lydia and Jan arrive back home in the Angelic Realm again, the Earth will already be in turmoil. In the meantime, it is imperative that the righteous and uninitiated are helped in every possible way – and there are so many friends ready and willing to receive help. You are acquainted with several!

"Without the slightest hint of being what you would call 'religious,' I must earnestly emphasize that behind everything is the Father, who wants to set everything right. The Father, First Source, the Great Spirit, that you mostly call 'God,' is neither Mohammed nor Buddha nor Jehovah – nor any other such deity under various names, who sits in some remote celestial pocket to judge, reprove, and condemn. There is only one God and Mother/Father – and until this is recognized and accepted over the entire Earth, there can be no peace. A revolution is required to attain this – and a revolution you shall receive!

"Exactly how this is to come about I am not yet at liberty to divulge. Since the planets of the Universe apply unarmed combat, the Earth will be taken completely by surprise. Slowly but surely the people will come to understand there really is an inhabited Universe, that there are more human-like beings than you who wish you no harm. You are afraid, but have no need to be. So much dread and terror is spread via your media that a completely different attitude must be adopted. They hold power, but they must transform it to something good. Love is the password that will shine down on you from the blue firmament you call Heaven. Love shall rule your entire world and preserve the Earth's magnificent, incomparable beauty from now on. Everyone will sing of Love, speak of Love, whisper about Love, shout about Love, show Love, and smile in Love to one another."

"How will racism, promiscuity, and other grievances be eliminated? Does anyone really give two hoots about words?" asked Lydia.

"Not just words, my dear; so much else will come to pass," assured Lady Nada. "The wicked will not manage to survive on Earth any longer. For their part, it will all be over, and those of them who do not die will be exiled to another planet. There are lots and lots of planets, as the pair of you may have noticed. What you have seen is but a drop in the ocean; there are many, many more."

"There has to be another sort of music introduced on Earth, too," interjected Lanto-Pilgrim. "In Agartha, one is blessed with hearing the most beautiful music, but as soon as one moves up above the surface, one's ears are invaded by the most horrible din of jarring, rowdy, unfriendly noise, depicting music in some primitive form of carnal sensuality, in the worst possible sense."

Both Lydia and I agreed wholeheartedly.

"The Earth will be restored to how it was intended," said Saint Germain. "It was created in sublime beauty and will again return to that former beauty in abundance! The Earth will be a place where Friends like to amble: Friends with one another, Friends with others and – above all – Friends with themselves. One of Earth's greatest deficiencies is the inability to love oneself. It would seem so very hard for people to feel happy about themselves and what they do. Humans punish themselves through their lack of love and incapacity to accept one another.

196

"This is an area we desperately need help with. The mass media ought to be instrumental in helping, but they don't want to. That must also be radically changed."

"There certainly is much to do," I commented. "How does one bring comfort to the comfortless people?"

"It can be done," professed Lanto. "Lissa is a terrific comforter, and there are others just like her. All humans should have a pet; animals can teach them an enormous amount. Animals do have souls, even if there are many who say otherwise. Some of them have individual souls, just like people, while others have collective souls."

Lydia and I were unanimous in our agreement. We are, after all, friends with Pan!

"Indeed! And speaking of Pan," interjected El Morya, quite out of the blue, "it is furthermore intended that when the Earth has undergone its metamorphosis and had its beauty-sleep, Nature's Elementals will exist visibly there. This will be a great help to you, as it will be impossible for people to deny their existence when they can see them with their very own physical eyes."

"The Earth will not be divided up into countries, as the map of the World now shows," boomed Melchizesdek's powerful voice. "A completely new order will come about, with total co-operation, just like on the other planets, which will give your mass media something else to think about than wickedness and scandals. Furthermore, dear children, you should know that we are not speaking of this happening in a hundred years' time, but soon, very soon indeed – which is why this book has to be written."

"People do not care and will not bother to care," I intervened wearily. I become so sad whenever I think about our beautiful Earth, which I still consider my home. Lydia must have been on the same wavelength, for I saw her eyes were moist with tears.

Melchizedek arose and exclaimed, "There is only one word that applies to the entire planet Earth, and that word is LOVE!"

The five Masters stood up and formed a circle around Lydia and me. They all joined hands.

My very last glimpse of Earth was Lissa's ragged, happily waving tail, signifying the flagship that, with infinite speed, carried us back to the Heavenly Spheres.

32. Epilogue

Jan's message to the readers of this book:

This is my last visit of this type to Earth. Both my friend Lydia and I have received new directives from other "latitudes." To Lydia's infinite delight, Lanto-Pilgrim has given her a puppy. He was so deeply moved by her great love for his own Lissa, that when the latter gave birth to a litter of puppies in Agartha, at the Inner Earth, he took one of them up to our Heavenly Spheres – an adorable little bitch, which Lydia instantly christened Lillissa.

We must say farewell to all further contact with the Earth in the form I have conveyed. There is so much that is about to happen with this planet – changes for the better, so that I perhaps may actively participate in these changes and be able once again to see the Earth, which has carried me for so long on her lush, beautiful surface. But in the meantime there are many ugly spots there that we must remove. When the winds of change storm over you, dear readers, remember that both Nature and humankind will be given the greatest beauty treatment, equal to none.

We have been on travels in the Universe. It is now time for us to ride on the Rays of Truth into the beginning of Infinity without end.

Appendix:
Concerning Zero Point Energy

Generally speaking, one can say that Zero Point Energy is the perpetual sea of energy that permeates all physicality – in fact, all creation; not only the higher, subtle planes, but also all physical planes.

Are there several planes of existence with differing living conditions? And, if this is so, one may ask: Is there a common denominator for life's manifestation on these planes? Perhaps then it isn't so strange that the majority of contemporary physicists – whether they adhere to the quantum physicists, "Newton-Einstein" factions, or string theory theoreticians – deny the existence of this energy.

However, there are scientists who assent to the concept of Zero Point Energy, whom I would call "Tomorrow's Physicists." Their conceptual world embraces not only several planes of existence, but also superluminal speeds, infinitely exceeding the speed of light, and an all-intersecting energy. These physicists work on the abstraction that scientifically explains how "to see a world in a grain of sand and a heaven in a wild flower, hold infinity in the palm of your hand, and eternity in an hour" (*William Blake*).

With these thought-provoking words, I shall now go on to attempt to explain what Zero Point Energy is.

In the same way it was believed during the Middle Ages that the Earth was completely flat, so has Space been conceived as a great void: just an enormous vacuum, bereft of any contact between the celestial bodies.

In the seventeenth century, scientists started experimenting with "recreating" Space. They believed that if they removed all gas from a vessel, it became completely emptied when it became vacuous. Then this reconstructed the state one thought to be Space.

During the nineteenth century, however, it became increasingly clear that kinetic energy, energy of motion, was present within the vacuum. This gave rise to the idea that if one chilled this evacuated vessel down to absolute zero (minus 273°C), the thermal radiation would thereby be removed. However, when absolute zero was successfully achieved, it was discovered that the radiation still remained present – i.e., the energy continued to exist inside the vacuum even at absolute zero.

This energy, or these particles, constantly surrounds us, and we all are linked together via them. Another characteristic of the particles is that they exchange information many times faster than the speed of light. It was through these experiments that science, via quantum mechanics and quantum physics, was able to prove the existence of this "something" that creates an imminent link and a connection direct from the one to the other independent of distance – to put it in layman's terms.

Predecessors within Zero Point Energy (ZPE)

The greatest of them all is, without a shadow of a doubt, the inventor and engineer *Nikola Tesla* (1856-1943), who was born in Serbia, but worked in the USA for many years. It was he who made the use of electricity commercially viable, and his principles are the foundation of all electronics and electrical applications we have today. He even invented devices driven by Zero Point Energy, which were effectively opposed and thwarted – and still awaiting introduction for use in our society.

Several inventors, both before and after Tesla, recognized the strong connection between consciousness and science. They realized that the conscious thought was a part of the scientific equation they had made it their lives' work to solve. We find an early forerunner in *Christiaan Huygens* (1629-1695), a Dutch alchemist, mathematician, astronomer, physicist, and author ("Light consists of waves").

Among the great names after Tesla, we find an American, Dr. *Henry Moray* (1892-1974), inventor of the "Moray Valve," a device that draws "Radiant Energy" from "Energy Waves of the Universe." Dr. Moray further spoke of a boundless sea of energy that surrounds and permeates all creation. Also, he saw a connection between electricity and consciousness.

What are Zero Point Energy (ZPE) and Zero Point Field (ZPF)?

As you almost certainly have come to understand by all that has been mentioned hitherto, this is no easily captured energy, with the limited knowledge and intellectual capacity mankind currently possess. To give an analogy: It would be rather like trying to weigh a bucket full of water while standing at the bottom of the sea.

Zero Point Energy is the energy of the energies, if you know what I mean. It is namely the base of all other expressions of energy; it builds up everything, from the most subtle manifestations to the more blatant. Sheldan Nidle refers to it as the "Creation Energy."

A significant property, which is hard for the majority of the world's established academics to accept, is that Zero Point Energy is conscious. It is able to both manifest its "own" intention or objective and to support the intention or objective of a more complex energy (e.g., a focused thought, a directed thought energy).

Since ZPE is a conscious energy, and is the foundation and building blocks of all manifestations, this indicates that all matter is conscious, and all expressions of energy have consciousness – from sunlight to tree radiation and uranium ore's radioactivity. The poet William Blake correctly referred to an animate nature, even if in this article we prefer to speak of directed, conscious thought or intention. Eastern philosophy calls ZPE "Prana" and "Ki," which attributes a more spiritual connotation.

As we have concluded, to underpin ZPE using other tools would be something of a fool's errand, since everything is composed of ZPE. We ought to therefore instead concentrate on signifying the characteristics, traits, effects, and the potentialities for making practical use of this abundance of basic energy.

But first, a few words about Zero Point Field.

Look at ZPF as a net wherein ZPE floats, is coordinated, and kept in place – a sort of mold or matrix, existing in both the micro-environment and the macro. You may perhaps have seen a Kirlian photograph of a leaf, which depicts the energy aura radiating out from the leaf's outline? An interesting observation is that if you cut off a part of the leaf and re-take the photograph, the new photograph shows that the original energy field remains intact, the "mold"/ZPF is not affected – it is evidently held intact on a different plane.

So what came first: the chicken or the egg? – the energy or the field? The answer is probably of no consequence. The field organizes the energy and allows it to materialize on a lower plane of existence. Take yourself, for example: Around and within you is a matrix that attracts, organizes and controls the Zero Point Energy inside the myriad life processes, constantly occurring in your body. The portals through which ZPE from higher dimensions flows into your matrix, into your aura to become manifest, are usually referred to as the *chakras,* thirteen of which are considered to be greater and more powerful.

Another example of Kirlian photographs illustrating how that the matrix remains intact is where a hand has been amputated.

Properties and Characteristics

In this section I shall describe a few special features and distinguishing attributes more in terms of allegations than evidence. Evidence in the old-fashioned sense, i.e., academically conclusive, has no bearing here and in some instances is totally absent. However, you have ready access to evidence far more compatible with this subject, evidence which is as swift as ZPE itself, i.e., the immediate, intuitive response from your heart! Heed it, for no better evidence than this may be found.

- ZPE is a scalar wave. A scalar wave is a five-dimensional standing wave, a Zero Point Energy on a 5D level. Scalar waves have no "tensors" (i.e., no dimensions, heights, breadths or lengths). Does this sound odd? What it means is that ZPE, purely physically, is an infinitesimal point that does not spread out into any direction in the third dimension, and that a scalar wave is not measurable in 3D.

- Indeed, these non-linear waves do exist in 5D, where there is no space and time in the linear way we perceive them in 3D. But their effect becomes significantly apparent in our 3D existence, where they exist as an ultra-high electromagnetic frequency.

- Zero Point Energy is a consciously creative energy that exists everywhere and pervades all dimensions, from the higher, non-physical, to the lower, physical ones.

- Zero Point Energy turns particles into waves and scalar waves into particles.

- Modern physics cannot explain what exists in 95% of the Universe and how it affects the other 5%. All matter is created out of ZPE. All physicality is connected with everything else in the Universe; everything is linked to everything.

- Experimentally, via quantum mechanics and quantum physics, science has proven the existence of this "something" that links all things together and is able to exchange information at superluminal speed.

- A brief summary: Zero Point Energy is a formless, infinite energy – it exists in limitless supply, it is vastly faster than light and has extreme energy density. Zero Point Energy within an area the size of a proton is equivalent to the entire mass of the Universe. The atom is 99.99% "empty space," filled with ZPE (source: Lanna Mingo, BS and MS).

- Zero Point Energy is essentially responsible for the stability of atoms.

How then does Zero Point Energy flow between the dimensions?

If we continue limiting ourselves to the flow from 5D to 3D, from the higher physical fifth dimension to our dimension, this has earlier been addressed by us regarding humans. The exchange or transport into the physical body takes place via portals in the ethereal body, i.e., via the *chakra system*. It is here that the transition between the dimensions of this ultra-high-density energy frequency occurs.

But how does this look at the macro level? How does ZPE enter into our world? Well the answer is through actual "star gates" or "star portals." If you go to the following link: www.missionignition.net/bethe/ you will find illustrations with lines crossing the planet's surface. These lines are called ley lines, and the intersections or nodes are sometimes called star gates, which serve as enormous portals or doors that open and close. When these star gates open up, sometimes a time warp, or time distortion, occurs. In some of the more powerful portals, they are occasionally known as triangles (e.g., The Bermuda Triangle), where rather strange things are reported to have happened. People who have been there have experienced rotations similar to that of a tornado and a peculiar type of fog. When the star gate is shut or in a neutral position, it is possible to safely fly over or sail across the area without anything happening. But when the gate opens, the previously mentioned time warp is likely to occur.

Via these nodes, these portals, Zero Point Energy enters into our world and creates all we see around us. We can therefore say that matter is compressed light, and the light we can see with our naked eyes is also ZPE that has come down from 5D to our 3D reality through these very gates or portals.

The Ten Main Portals on Earth

These portals are positioned 19.5 degrees north and south of the Equator, five on either side. When Zero Point Energy flows through these portals into our reality, part of its effect maintains the Earth's ability to rotate and keeps it stable. The portals do not only warp the concept of time as they open, they open and close in sequence in order to, among other things, maintain the rotation and stability of our planet. If this doesn't indicate Zero Point Energy as a bearer of intelligence, I don't know what can!

Black Holes, Dark Matter, and Dark Energy

From humans, via Earth, out into Space. Here we face three new concepts: black holes, dark matter, and dark energy.

According to contemporary physicists, a black hole is a body mass in the Universe with uniquely powerful gravitation, making it impossible for either light or anything else to escape its bounds. Does this seem feasible?

By, among other things, studying the movement of the stars, one can conclude that there must be something more out there that one cannot see, something we call *dark matter.*

Is it not more logical to assume that black holes are gigantic star gates through which Zero Point Energy flows into our reality from the higher dimensions, and it is this energy that maintains the dynamics and stability of galaxies and stars? ZPE has such an enormously high frequency that it cannot be perceived with our naked eyes or today's technology; all becomes black. Doesn't this sound more feasible?

Practical Applications of Zero Point Energy

Let us roughly divide some of the practical uses in question into three groups, depending on which fraction of ZPE is relevant:

* Para Electrical Energy
* Healing Energy
* Life Force Energy

Para Electrical Energy. This type of energy chiefly concerns supplying "household electricity" to appliances in the home, besides generating power to offices, factories, and society in general. Prototypes exist. Much of its development has been kept secret and suppressed by powerfully influential forces in society, who deem this new technology a threat to their own position of influence, largely built on controlling the Earth's exploitable sources of fossil fuels.

It is highly likely that we happily shall see the breakdown of this power base over the next few years, enabling new sound and healthy technology based on para electrical energy to spring forth, forming the cornerstones of an innovative, hale and healthy society.

Generally one can say that Zero Point Energy has unlimited number of practical uses, e.g., as the energy source for the propulsion system of a spaceship, to name one which might cause you to raise your eyebrows and broaden your mind. To refute the existence of such spaceships is nothing anyone having seriously made a study of this subject would do. Solely those stupendously magnificent, complicated, and highly informative imprints in the cornfields, i.e., crop circles, are evidence enough to convince most. The spaceships utilize the unlimited supply of ZPE and transform the super high-frequency light into many dimensions and fractions. Their propulsion is built on the force of attraction between self-generated energy fields.

Since the technique relies on the advanced technology of a higher dimension where, among other things, time, distance, and inertia can be eliminated, it is currently still difficult for us to comprehend. However, it may help you a little on the way if you study the video clip at the following YouTube link: www.youtube.com/watch?v=XsuYH1qrBLg

Healing Energy. There are some tools available, albeit only a few so far, which introduce Zero Point Energy healing frequencies and help restore homeostasis, i.e., the balance, in the body. Among these practical devices the AM Wand and other devices can be mentioned. A more detailed product presentation may be found at the following two links: www.zeropointglobal.com and www.wandtheworld.com.

Life Force Energy. The difference between this type and healing energy is minuscule, but the devices that utilize this frequency range act to strengthen your bio-field, your aura. When your bio-field is strong, it protects against all forms of electronic "smog": radiation from mobile telephones, computers, power cables, etc. Wearing special bracelets or, above all, pendants, will give protection. Currently leading the market in this field are AM Pendants that work by resonating with and activating ZPE in all directions. This serves to organize and reinforce your bio-electric-field and restore your homeostasis to its natural, balanced state.

In these and similar applications, devices exist that can eliminate pain and invigorate people, improve the health of animals, make plants grow quicker and larger, besides enriching the nourishment content in food. Furthermore, the improvement of mental health may be achieved by applying the correct frequency of ZPE. People may feel calmer, more relaxed, happy, and joyful, in addition to sleeping more soundly.

The General Consensus of Contemporary Physicists

Even if an ever-increasing number of physicists are becoming curiously keen to carry out research into Zero Point Energy, they are still very much in a minority. The majority deny its existence and don't feel any inkling of being on the brink of a revolutionary paradigm shift.

An important distinction is that today's physicists cannot accept that energy can be conscious; they neither concede that intelligent intent is a main component, nor that we are dealing with an intelligent energy and that ZPE is what maintains an intelligent Universe. Quite to the contrary, it is considered by the majority of contemporary physicists that all matter is dead.

Modern physics is of the opinion that a field of energy is incapable of creating an effect at greater distances, if there is no matter within which to create an effect. If no matter exists, they are quite bewildered.

As has already been mentioned: modern physics cannot explain what exists in 95% of the Universe and how it affects the other 5%.

More on the Physics of Tomorrow

There is another science swiftly gaining ground, which clearly opposes much in the string theory and much associated with it and also opposes that which is closely aligned with most theories within modern theoretical physics. We allude to a science with increasing awareness that acknowledges the consciousness of Zero Point Energy, a science that proclaims we ought to look beyond Newton or Einstein, or even quantum physics – and instead should focus on developing a new science which describes the true nature of our physical reality.

This new science or physics is one of fractals, of helixes, one that views the entire process from a completely different angle, seeing consciousness as a part – a supportive component – and encompasses all of this in the science of physics.

As enlightenment increases, so too will the need for a paradigm shift intensify, and we will advance to the conscious physics as mentioned here. The traditionally established physics demand objective measurements; i.e., if it cannot be measured, then it does not exist. But many, a few of whom have been named in this compilation, have concluded with vibrant confirmation that this energy actually exists, and further managed to measure it. Consequently, we do have a physical foundation stone that both can and has been measured. It can be utilized by mankind to create an updated science, one that even embraces the non-physical reality. This new science may befittingly be included in a greater context, namely within the science of consciousness – a science that combines the physical aspects with the science of life.

[This appendix is an excerpt from an article written by *Karl-Gustav Levander,* who derived inspiration and factual information from Sheldan Nidle's DVD-lecture, "Zero Point, The Endless Sea of Energy" (www.paoweb.com), among other sources.]

Made in the USA
Las Vegas, NV
20 January 2023

65977904R00118